Praise for *Andrew Vachss*

"Many writers try to cover the same ground as Vachss. A handful are good. None are better."
—*People*

"Vachss's stories don't feature pointless bloodshed. Instead, they burn with righteous rage and transfer a degree of that rage to the reader."
—*The Washington Post Book World*

"Strong, gritty, gut-bucket stuff, so unsparing and vivid that it makes you wince. Vachss knows the turf and writes with a sneering bravado."
—*Chicago Tribune*

"Gritty, frightening, compelling and ultimately satisfying."
—*The Plain Dealer*

"Vachss's tough guy writing style grabs you by the hair and jerks you to attention."
—*Detroit Free Press*

"Gripping, unusual, and exciting."
—*Nashville City Paper*

ANDREW VACHSS

BLACKJACK

Andrew Vachss is a lawyer who represents children and youths exclusively. He is the author of many novels, including the Burke series, numerous stand-alones, and three collections of short stories. His work has been translated into twenty languages, and has appeared in *Parade*, *Antaeus*, *Esquire*, *Playboy*, and *The New York Times*, among other publications. He divides his time between his native New York City and the Pacific Northwest.

www.vachss.com

BLACKJACK

ANDREW VACHSS

BLACKJACK

A Cross Novel

VINTAGE CRIME/BLACK LIZARD
Vintage Books
A Division of Random House, Inc.
New York

A VINTAGE CRIME/BLACK LIZARD ORIGINAL, JULY 2012

Copyright © 2012 by Andrew Vachss

All rights reserved. Published in the United States by Vintage Books,
a division of Random House, Inc., New York.

Vintage is a registered trademark and Vintage Crime/Black Lizard
and colophon are trademarks of Random House, Inc.

Cross™ and all prominent characters featured herein are
trademarks of Andrew Vachss.

The Cataloging-in-Publication Data is on file at the Library of Congress.

ISBN: 978-0-307-94957-8

www.weeklylizard.com

www.vachss.com

Printed in the United States of America
10 9 8 7 6 5 4 3 2

for Georg Schmidt

husband to the lovely Sibylle, sire of The Mighty Nicolas
the first (and finest) translator of my books into German

You went out on your shield
a warrior to the end
I expected nothing less

And I'll see you soon enough, old friend

BLACKJACK

THE LION'S full-maned magnificence filled the glass of the high-power telescopic sight. Accustomed to domination of all he sees, the beast was unaware that what he does *not* see was now holding him captive.

His captor dialed in with great care—only a perfectly placed shot would preserve the trophy he had paid so much to take. The lion was no menacing figure to the human cradling the rifle—he regarded himself as the king of a very different jungle, one much more vicious and far less forgiving.

To this man, the lion was a mere *objet d'art*: destined to become still another symbol of his elite standing, its value enhanced by difficulty of acquisition. Any man can *buy* things; only those of a special breed may grant themselves permission to *take* things. And what better way to illustrate the difference than to display those trophies they have taken with their own hands?

The title "King of the Jungle" had been reduced to ultimate irony. The lion's multi-generational belief that he was master of all he surveyed had become an illusion. In reality, he was nothing but a mere target for an impending hostile takeover.

The sight's crosshairs intersected on the lion's vital

organs—a head shot would destroy the trophy. The scope was mounted on a custom-built .458 Weatherby Magnum, the rifle itself bolted onto a tripod with its own click-adjustment capability. A separate range-finder–and–windage-meter combination was mounted within its housing. The rifle's heavy, non-reflective barrel protruded through a mesh netting covering the open sunroof of a khaki-and-beige Land Rover.

If the lion knew an enemy was approaching, he would follow the natural sequence of his breed: first warn, then attack. But he had no such knowledge. Instead, he rested comfortably in the restorative sun, waiting for the female members of his pride to make a kill. The beast remained unaware that he had been reduced to a potential trophy from the moment the hunter's kill-shot had been dialed in.

The hunter was dressed in couture jungle gear: knee-high black boots and matching cartridge belt topped with a leopard-banded bush hat. He stood frozen behind the scope, visualizing as would any artist picturing in his mind what he would create on the blank canvas before him. As always, this master artist's preferred medium was blood.

"Isn't he perfect?" the artist gloated. "Here, take a look for yourself."

A woman's head slowly emerged through the opening. A pink chiffon scarf covered her long blonde hair; another protected her throat. She was well aware that every asset she possessed was depreciating, so she guarded them all with extreme care, knowing that plastic surgery would, eventually, become self-mockery.

She slid closer to the man, calculating every movement, knowing her role was to be another of his trophies, always on display. Delicately, she peered through the scope, taking care not to let it actually touch her extended eyelashes.

"Oh, he *is* a beauty. I'll bet he has his pick of the whole herd."

"Pride."

"What?"

"Pride. That's what they call a herd of lions, a pride."

"Oh."

"You have to understand the culture of this area, Celia," the artist pontificated. "That's the only way you can truly appreciate the thrill of the hunt."

"I see . . ." she murmured, gently placing her hand on the man's forearm arm as she gazed adoringly into his eyes. These seemingly spontaneous moves had been practiced and polished since her early teens, and perfected well before her first marriage.

Two natives squatted on the ground, grateful for the meager shade provided by the faux-camo Land Rover. They exchanged glances but did not speak. Like the woman, they had fully internalized their role many years ago; their every word and gesture honed by constant practice.

"He's a man-eater," the great white hunter said.

Celia checked her husband's face for hint of a double-entendre. Detecting none, she quickly ran her tongue over her lips, taking care not to speak.

"No question about it, he's the one. Killed three of their people so far, and I've got the documents to prove it. You know why that lion is so nice and relaxed? This whole area is reserved for photo-safaris. No hunting allowed. The only exception is when the government certifies that a *particular* animal has become dangerous to man."

"Aren't they *all* dangerous?"

"Only if they leave the preserve. And why should they do that? They've got everything they need right here: plenty of food, clean water, a goodly supply of game . . . you name it. If you lived at the Four Seasons, why would you ever check into a Motel 6?"

"Then how is this one different?"

"He's not," the man said, his voice a life raft bobbing on a perfect ocean of confidence. "*I* am. The 'president' of this so-called country is actually the owner—everything inside the borders belongs to him.

"You understand?" the man continued, glancing at the woman to make certain she missed none of the implications of his speech. "This country is his *property*. If you own something, you can sell it. Or rent it. But there's nothing left for him to sell anymore, not from *this* country. Half the population's already dead. Natural causes, like starvation and disease. There's no infrastructure at all, no way to distribute food or even seed. It could have been a paradise, but President-for-life Qranunto never understood even the simplest business principles. Now it's impossible for that maniac to get his hands on hard currency."

"He must have *some*—"

"Money? Sure. He *did*. But now it's all gone. Sitting in banks all around the world. Billions. But he can't get his hands on it."

"If it's in his name, why not just take it out?"

"Because he has no one he could trust, so he set everything up so that he'd have to show up in person to claim it. And he's wanted by every country on the planet. The UN, the World Court, even whatever useless organization they have for Africa, they all have him under an arrest-on-sight order. If he wants any money in his hands, he has to have someone come over here and *put* it there."

"Oh."

"'Oh' is right, baby. Cost me one-point-five million. That's in euros, not dollars. For that, I get the run of the place. That's why we're using the Land Rover. What we're doing isn't some stupid 'safari'—in fact, it's not about hunting at all."

"It's not?"

"No," he replied, in the same smug voice he used when a casino employee kowtowed to him—as a well-known "whale," he was courted and comped by every legal gambling establishment from Vegas to Monte Carlo. "When you hunt for trophies, there's all kinds of stupid rules about how to do it. But when you're hunting for food, there's never any rules."

"We're not going to *eat* that thing, are we? I mean—"

"Just listen!" the man abruptly halted whatever foolishness was about to come out of that ripe mouth of hers. Well within his rights, was he not? A man owns what he pays for, and those top-drawer collagen injections hadn't come cheap.

"Some trophies *are* food. Not the kind of food you live on, the kind of food that lets you live any way you choose. When I walk into a boardroom, why do you think the others stand up? I'll tell you why: because they know what I can do. They know what I'm capable of. And it's trophies like that incredible creature over there that *prove* it."

♣

CELIA REARRANGED her lips into a fetching pout. This wasn't the first such lecture she'd endured, and she had known what a trophy wife's role was years before she'd signed her first pre-nup. Not her fault if *this* Master of the Universe believed her story about how the "traumatic ectopic pregnancy" she had endured in her early teens had left her permanently scarred, both internally and emotionally. When she had tearfully disclosed her secret, the hunter had feigned some degree of sympathy. But he could hardly keep the self-satisfied smirk off his face when she explained that those endless surgeries had finally resulted in a complete hysterectomy—she could never give him children.

His lawyers had repeatedly warned that even the most ironclad of pre-nups would not protect him financially were he to father a child. With that possibility removed—"damage capped," as his lawyers phrased it—the man acquired a new possession. A *safe* new possession, allowing him to happily discard his supply of condoms.

A vasectomy had been out of the question. His seed was too valuable to destroy. It would continue the line of superior beings long after his death—arrangements had already been made, and paid in full.

The possibility that Celia would cheat on him—thus exposing him to a sexually transmitted disease—was nonexistent. He did not overtly restrict her movements, but those who were paid to shadow her around the clock had never reported misconduct of any kind, much less a sexual encounter.

And they were well aware of the penalty for touching what did not belong to them.

So the hunter knew everything about Celia—what she did, who she did it with, where she did it. The mansion was fully wired for audio and video, all phone lines were set to record both incoming and outgoing, and she shopped only with credit cards, so all purchases could be monitored. And even if Celia somehow managed to build a secret supply of cash, she could not have bought a throw-away cell phone without his shadow employees noticing.

Of course, some activities could not be *completely* monitored. Her monthly visit to the gynecologist to check the internal scarring never took long—and keeping the wife of this man waiting was out of the question.

Her physician understood her state of mind, and always had a pre-filled prescription on hand. Celia's fear of uterine cancer from what she always called "that butchering" required moderate daily doses of Somaso, a mild anti-anxiety drug.

The contents of those prescription bottles did not match

their labels. Celia's only actual anxiety was that she might forget her daily dose of Implan, the most powerful fertility drug on the market.

Celia's owner was blissfully unaware of this monumental bait-and-switch. But if Celia's plan worked out, he'd know soon enough.

The doctor had warned her about the dangers of the new drug. Hypocritical little twit, glad enough to take the stack of hundred-dollar bills Celia handed over each time, but still wanting to protect himself from malpractice lawsuits in case the child was born defective in any way. *As if!* Celia sneered internally. The fool apparently didn't know that providing care for a congenitally defective child not only was extremely expensive, but, properly handled, could turn into a lifelong and *very* substantial annuity.

The high-priced lawyer Celia had consulted before the marriage had not charged her for the advice, or for providing the name of a physician willing to risk anything for money to feed his own addiction. No record of her visit to either man existed.

The man with the rifle was no different from so many others Celia had known, but there was a core-deep meanness about him that set her perfect teeth on edge. That cruelty surfaced when he affectionately called her "Cee" in front of company. *Only* in front of company, making sure they all knew that "Cee" was really "C." And what that single letter stood for. As if she needed still another reminder that she was a possession, and where her only value resided.

Despite her best efforts at disguising it, Celia had the feral intelligence of any successful predator. Hardly a genius on any IQ scale perhaps, but crafty enough to understand that a narrow mind could also be a focused one. So she was careful not to overdo her interest every time the man she had married explained how the world *really* works.

Again.

"And the biggest trophy of all is a killer," he droned on. "When you kill a killer, all his kills belong to you. That's what makes the world go around, Celia. Numbers. *Big* numbers."

Celia felt the man's words throbbing between her legs. She always had an instantly intimate response to big numbers. Not to the concept, to the reality.

Numbers can turn into money, and money can forge a sword that can cut with either edge. After all, aren't those of *her* tribe measured? Aren't *their* numbers constantly monitored and compared? And, when acquired, do not such measurements enhance those of the man who owns them?

Anyone can learn to shoot relatively well. Anyone can learn to recognize targets. But only the most skillful hunters come to truly *know* their prey.

♣

A PRESENCE darker than the shadow between the two natives moved, a tiny dot writhing with life. But although raised from birth to know every sight, sound, and smell of the savannah, the natives sensed no change in their immediate environment.

Over a mile away, a lone acacia tree stood, its roots reaching deep into the parched soil. It might be a trick of the blazing sun, but an indistinct blur seemed to move within the acacia's trunk, as though the tree itself were widening. A pair of tiny crossbows poked carefully out of the blur, as if mocking the hunter's camouflaged rifle barrel.

If the natives had been able to tune in to the blob of shadow between them, they would have heard the words "big numbers," repeated in an ancient version of their own language. Translated, those words would form a single command:

"Hit."

Instantly, the eye of the hunter and the sternum of his purchased yet predatory wife were simultaneously and soundlessly penetrated by trident-shaped arrows.

The kills were soundless and without impact. Man and wife never changed position, as if frozen in place by death.

The natives understood patience to be a vital part of their jobs. But after more than three hours of uncharacteristic silence from the sniper's perch above them, they dared to sneak a look at where the hunter had been perched.

What they saw was enough for them to exchange a single glance, drop lightly to the ground, untie their sacks of provisions, strap on their rifles, and start walking.

It would take weeks for them to reach their home, and surviving such a trek was anything but guaranteed. But driving the Land Rover back themselves would create too great a mystery, and they knew exactly how such mysteries are always solved.

The long march would give them plenty of time to agree upon a story. A logical, possible story, not the impossibility of what they had actually observed.

Among their tribe, to be perceived as insane was a death sentence. Neither man spoke of the two playing cards protruding from the chest pocket of the hunter's safari jacket: the ace of clubs and the jack of spades.

Neither ever would.

♣

IN A part of town closed to all but those who would be regarded as outsiders anywhere else, a tall, slender Latino lounged against a freshly whitewashed wall. His pose was highly stylized, practiced in private years prior to any display in public. Years in which he had no access *to* the public.

The Latino spread his duster-length black coat like

raven's wings. Behind him was gang-turf graffiti, elaborately spray-painted, transforming the wall into a billboard. One with a very clear message.

The graffiti was pristine. That it had not been over-tagged was a bold proclamation that the wall stood within undisputed territory.

The Latino slouched to enable his arm to more comfort-ably encircle the bulging waist of an obviously pregnant *chola* . . . a lovely young girl, only a year past the elaborate *quinceañera* for which her parents had saved since her birth. If they had been unhappy at her choice of a date for such a special event, they never gave the slightest sign. There were many reasons for this.

The girl's long dark hair set off a Madonna's face, aglow with impending motherhood. The man's cowboy hat had been custom-made from skins of the Gila monster. It both shielded his eyes and veiled their message. His long duster was casually draped over a candy-orange silk shirt buttoned only at the throat, the better to display a single heavy-linked gold chain.

Soon a diamond would be added to that chain—the baby his woman was expecting would be his first.

A candy-orange '64 Impala stood arrogantly at the curb. A two-door hardtop with rectangular black panels inset on the hood, roof and trunk, each intricately over-painted in a delicate white floral pattern, the quintessential low-rider was fully dropped to the limit of its air-bag suspension.

The Latino's pose was a perfect, albeit unconscious, imi-tation of the Great White Hunter's. Whatever he surveyed, he owned.

Under the hat's brim, his eyes swept the street, relentless as a prison searchlight. He registered the approach of three young men, but kept his face expressionless.

One of the trio had covered his head with a candy-orange

do-rag. Another sported long black hair tied behind him in a ponytail and held in place by a headband, also displaying the gang's color. The third was a heavily muscled individual in a candy-orange wife-beater T-shirt. His head was freshly shaven, glistening in the sun.

Let other gangs fly multi-colors, *Los Peligrosos* needed only one to distinguish itself. Various tattoos marked them as well, obedient to the decades-old tradition of "ink to link."

To wear the gang's color without its name permanently etched in one's body would have been unthinkable. Flying gang colors might be prohibited inside the prisons which awaited them all and disgorged some, but they would carry their skin-branding to the grave. Although they never spoke it aloud, all knew that their life offered only one final alternative to incarceration—a ceremonious burial.

The tall man took a long, ostentatious toke from the cigarillo-blunt in his left hand. He did not offer a hit to his woman—she was pregnant, how would that look? As he patted the *chola*'s bulging belly, his left hand brushed the outline of a semi-automatic pistol in his coat pocket. Touching his future with each hand, not knowing which would come first: birth or death.

The crew formed a rough circle, standing so that they could listen to their leader and watch the street at the same time.

Time passed, as it does in such places.

"You want to roll, you got to pay the toll," the tall man schooled the youth with the shaved head. "These streets test a man. You know this when you coming up, just making your first little baby-move. Me, now, I passed that test. I can *make* a life"—he bends, quickly and gracefully at the waist, to plant a showy kiss on his girl's belly—"and I can *take* a life. You hear me, *ese?*"

"Always hear you, *jefe*."

"I don't mind dying. That's what it takes, you want to be out here every day, walking with your head high, *sí?*"

"Dying comes quick out here," the youth wearing the headband solemnly intoned.

"So?" the tall man immediately challenged. "To die quickly, that is *nothing*. A sheep can be slaughtered, but a sheep cannot kill. So, when it dies, it is always a quick death.

"Only when you go Inside do you face that *final* test of a man. Inside, that is dying *slow*. Every day, dying. The days pass; nothing changes. The only thing that happens fast is when it comes time to stick a pig.

"But Inside, even a blade will not always mean death. I have seen men survive *thirty* stab wounds—in prison, that's the one thing the infirmary is good for. If you don't get wheeled in DOA, you probably live.

"Not out here. On the boulevard, you point your pistol, you pull the trigger, and death follows the bullets. Inside, to kill, you must be close to *el enemigo*. To shoot, yes, that takes heart. But to stab, that is what takes the heart, *verdado?*"

"*Sí, ese.*" The three acolytes spoke as one.

"Inside, just being there, you get old," their leader continued. "If you lucky. Out here, bang-bang! You live or you die. But in there, it is twenty-four/seven pain."

"I been Inside—" the youth with the headband started to speak.

"I know you have, *hermano*," the leader said. Although still young, he had learned that a vital part of his role was to provide support and encouragement. "I ain't downing you. But the Walls, it ain't like the kiddie camps. Only one game gets played in the Man's House. War. Race war. And there ain't no neutral ground. No place to get out the way.

"Out here, we fight among ourselves. Like fools, perhaps. But that is how it has always been. But in there, it does not matter—even united, we would never be strong enough. This ain't the West Coast, you feel me? It ain't even Chicago. So we outnumbered, very bad. Downstate, you look around, you see nothing but wrong colors. *Blancos y negros.* Nazis and Zulus. How you gonna ever be safe between those *psicópatas?* They try and wolf-pack you on the way back from Commissary, you expect that, no? So you never go to that window alone. But how can you protect yourself when you get jammed right in your own cell? Some of them, they so *loco* they even take you out standing on the mess line.

"And the yard . . . *pantano de la muerte!* They do their drive-bys walking! When that black-white thing gets hopping, even if we ever *could* outnumber them, there ain't no place for us but the middle—we still too busy fighting each other to see the truth. And you know what happens if you get caught in the middle: *crunch!*

"Body counts, that's like status for some of them maniacs, specially those Nazis. They already under a load of Life Withouts, so there's nothing to hold them in check. Even Ad Seg—fancy name they use for Solitary—that's always all full up, so what those psychos got to lose, a little yard time?

"No place to stash them *all*, so the COs just let them cruise around and do their thing. Which is making other people dead. They got, like, *contests*, man. One Nazi dude I heard about when I was in there, he had, like, thirteen kills. Confirmed kills."

A micron-thin shadow rippled faintly inside the elaborately painted panel on the hood of the low-rider. As in another jungle, on another continent, its presence was undetected.

If any of the group had been able to tune in to that throbbing shadow, they would have heard a faint whisper:

"Asesinatos confirmados."

From a rooftop several blocks away, a shape similar to that

which had emerged from the acacia tree formed itself from a pile of debris.

Suddenly, the girl twitched as if from a cold chill, her mother-to-be senses picking up . . . something. The leader patted her shoulder. "Don't worry, *mi amor*. I am here. With me, you *always* be safe."

The girl nodded as if reassured, but her hands remained clasped defensively across her stomach.

From the shadow, another one-word sentence, now in an Aztec language no longer spoken anywhere on earth. Translated, it would have been:

"Stay."

Unaware of his reprieve, the leader continued his lecture.

"Out here, a man don't be talking about who he took out, but it gets *known*. We not *Los Peligrosos* for nothing. You want to carry the brand, you got to take that *stand*, hear me?"

Unnoticed by all, the infamous "dead man's hand"—aces and eights—depicted on the white wall behind them incorrectly as a full house—had morphed: all the cards were now arranged correctly, but as duplicates, not pairs: the aces and eights, all in hearts.

♣

THE INTERIOR was a scaled-down version of a Pentagon war room: maps, charts, and graphs, blinking computer terminals, two long conference tables, angled so they formed a V, at the apex of which was a giant-screen LED monitor. On one side of the monitor was a series of Insta-Graph meters; on the other, a larger row of instruments with read-out dials. Next to the graphs and meters on each side stood a stack of CDs, all neatly labeled by the same process that slid them out every few minutes.

The room itself was underground and windowless. The

only sound was the whisper of the machines used to keep the computers at a constant temperature.

On the monitor: projected views of crime scenes, all slaughter-homicides.

Five people were present, their eyes fixed on the screen.

"What makes those Pentagon pussies so sure this guy knows any more than they do?" The speaker was a double-wide male—not especially tall, but almost frighteningly massive. His body lacked sharply defined muscle; it looked more like extruded power, stretching the man's skin to its limits. Even his black-and-gray hair appeared to be a tightly plastered cap.

The man was wearing a T-shirt, with a hard-plastic shoulder holster hanging under his left arm. The MAC-10 it carried looked like a toy against its bulky human backdrop.

"It won't hurt to hear him out. Just let him take a look at what we've got, Percy." The speaker was a slim, blond man, neatly dressed in agency-issue standard. Every aspect of his appearance was bland.

"He'll go along with our conditions?" a thickly built but very shapely woman with a mane of tiger-striped hair asked. She was wearing a one-piece spandex outfit, a pair of long, thin knives strapped to the outside of one thigh. That same thigh's muscle-flex was clearly visible as she swung one booted foot up onto the table.

"He's already on his way, Tiger," said a doll-faced Asian woman in a white lab coat. She held a clipboard in one hand, studying it closely through oversized round glasses. "That's confirmed, Tracker?"

The man she addressed simply nodded. He was an American Indian, with high, prominent cheekbones, red-bronze skin, jet-black hair, and dark, hooded eyes.

"Excellent, Wanda," the blond man said. "He's supposed to be the leading authority on serial killers. Not only solved a number of significant cases, but predicted their moves as well. The FBI wants nothing to do with him. Probably because he's publicly mocked their alleged 'profiles.'"

"This has got nothing, *nothing* to do with serial killers, damn it!" Percy barked out. "What the hell's wrong with these wimps? They want to *study* this thing? That ain't the answer to the problem."

"What *is* the answer?" Wanda asked, a wisp of a smile playing across her lips.

"The answer?" Percy grunted his disgust. "Same as it always is. We find it; we kill it. No different from what *it's* been doing all over the world. Am I right?" he demanded, opening his arms in a gesture meant to involve the whole room.

Only Tiger nodded in agreement.

A light glowed on a console in front of Wanda. "He's here," she said. "Everybody ready?"

Only the blond man responded. To Wanda, only the blond man mattered. She leaned forward, her mouth close to a tiny microphone, and whispered, "Bring him down."

♣

THE FOUR-INCH-THICK, bunker-style door opened slowly and silently. A short, husky man entered. He was in his fifties, with close-cropped hair, wearing slightly tinted glasses. His stride was that of a man heavily endowed with "no need to prove it" self-assurance.

Everybody in the room had been told what to expect: a top-tier professional, the best at what he did.

Tracker scanned for egotism; Tiger for her version of the same weakness. Percy performed a lightning-quick threat assessment, all three warriors operating on autopilot.

The blond man and Wanda simply waited.

The man did not enter alone—he was air-sandwiched between two others. One stepped ahead of him, the other close behind. Both were dressed in simple gray jumpsuits and matching watch caps. One carried a submachine gun in a sling, the other held a short-barreled semi-auto, blued against glare. Their faces were so alike they could be twins— human robots who would respond to only one source of orders, acting as a single unit.

At a nod from Wanda, they walked the man between them over to a waiting chair. He took the intentionally unsubtle hint and sat down, still not having said a word.

As if on cue, the two men backed out of the room, their weapons trained on the now seated man up to the moment the door closed.

"Thanks for coming, Doctor," the blond man said, not offering his hand.

"Glad to be of help."

"We'll see," Percy muttered, obviously unconvinced, and not disguising his skepticism.

Tiger gazed at the new arrival with measured intensity; Wanda consulted her clipboard. Tracker remained motionless.

Finally, the new arrival spoke. "You said you had something you wanted me to see. . . ."

"That is correct," the blond man responded. "Wanda?"

Wanda walked briskly to the giant monitor, prepared to hit a switch, and asked, "You've been briefed . . . ?"

"I believe I have," the consultant replied. "This is about the Canyon Killings, right?"

"Yes. You've seen the crime-scene photos?"

"Uh-huh. Same as these blowups over on that wall," he said, nodding at the poster-sized photos of demolished human remains.

Nobody made a sound.

"Roll it already," Percy snapped.

Wanda's long, lacquered nails floated over the console. On the ring finger of her left hand was the rarest of star sapphires: white, with a black star, set in platinum.

♣

THE MONITOR'S screen snapped into life. A white male—thin, with a receding hairline and matching chin, was smoking expansively, gesturing as if addressing a legion of adoring fans at a press conference. As the camera dollied in, it became clear that the man was clad in a prison jumpsuit, leg-cuffed to his chair.

The camera slowly pulled back to show viewers that the man was behind bars, but not in an individual cell. The blond man set the scene for the newly arrived consultant:

"This piece of fecal matter is one Mark Robert Towers. Thirty-seven. Habitual—no, make that *chronic*—offender. Priors include rape, abduction with intent, arson. Arrested four days ago by the locals.

"It wasn't a difficult case to crack, but the crime scene was unusually repulsive. Mother and daughter raped and killed in broad daylight—looked like a push-in burglary that went bad. Fortunately, the scumbag not only left his prints all over everything he touched, they vacuumed enough DNA out of the victims to put him down for the count.

"Death Row's a lock for this . . . whatever he is. Not here—Illinois is still in a mess after those mass no-execution orders issued by the Governor . . . before he went to prison himself. I believe that's something of a tradition in this state.

"That, however, is of no consequence. He's already DNA-tied to at least three more kills: two in Florida, one in Texas. All women. He's a dead man, and the clock is winding down."

"Clock?" Percy snorted. "You mean calendar, don't you? It takes longer to kill one of those maggots in this country than it would to rebuild the Pyramids with Lego blocks."

"That's not our assignment," the blond man said, his measured voice holding just a trace of condescension. "But *this* is. Last night, out of the blue, Towers said he wanted to make a statement about the Canyon Killings in California. They Miranda-ed him up and down, got it on video as well, but he insisted on confessing to the murders. All of them.

"That's what we have. His statement, nothing more. In a few more seconds, the volume will come up, you'll hear it for yourself."

The consultant assumed an attentive posture but remained silent. He apparently did not intend to take notes.

The sound came up on the monitor as the camera moved in tight on the speaker's face.

"First of all, you people need to understand that this business about me only killing women is absolute bullshit. I mean, there's no point in me not telling the truth *now*, is there?

"I'm a natural-born killer. Hell, I couldn't even begin to count how many people I've sent over to the other side. But that's got nothing to do with sex. I kill for the fun of it.

"See, it's like movies. No matter how much you like any one movie, it gets old after a while. So you watch a new one. What makes me special is that I don't watch movies; I *make* them. I'm not just the star; I'm the director.

"Don't matter to me where I am. When the mood hits me, I just go all red inside . . . and somebody dies. Walking Death, that's me. You people think you can understand *that?*"

An off-camera questioner asked: "You said you wanted to talk to us about the Canyon Killings?"

"Yeah, that's what I said. I got a lot more than those to talk about, too . . . if I feel like it."

Off-camera: "What does that mean, Mark?"

The speaker's posture tightened. His face narrowed in the anger he had carried throughout his adult life. "It means *respect*, that too complicated for you? Respect, that's all I'm asking for. I'm tired of being treated like crap. No cigarettes unless I ask one of the cops to come and light it for me. No TV, no mail. I can clear a lot of cases for you guys. All I expected was to be treated like a *man*, you know what I mean?"

Off-camera: "We'll do what we can."

"What's that supposed to mean? I got rights. Same rights as anyone else. Granny-killing niggers get treated better in here than *me?* I got a right to speak to the media if I want to. And what about my mail? You *know* you got no right to hold on to that."

Off-camera: "Your lawyer . . ."

"I don't need no two-bit Public Defender to be *my* lawyer. Once I get to tell my story, you best believe I'll have all the lawyers I need."

The screen flickered out, faded to black.

"This next tape was made a few hours later," the blond man said.

The consultant so far addressed only as "Doctor" just nodded, clearly waiting for more.

When Towers faced the camera again, his hair was freshly coiffed, and a full pack of cigarettes was by his elbow, along with a yellow legal pad and some sharpened pencils. He was still seated, but in a more comfortable chair. The leg cuffs had been removed.

"Then there was that time in Texas. Just outside of Houston, in this Lovers' Lane. I would've been satisfied with a straight-up robbery, but that kid had to try and get tough with me. After I did him, I couldn't very well leave the bitch around to be a witness, so I did her, too. That's my trademark: no witnesses. You check around, you'll see what I mean."

Off-camera: "The Canyon Killings . . . ?"

"Yeah, you want to get right to it, don't you? Okay, fair enough. Now that you're treating me like a white man, I'll give you what I said I would—I'm a man of my word. So listen: When you've been in prison, done as much time as I done, you know how the joints're full of punks trying to make a name for themselves. Big talkers, but it's just a bunch of stories they tell. It's enough to make a real man sick.

"Like that little weasel down in Florida, Bundy. Whining about how looking at pictures of naked women made him crazy and all. You know what? That one he said he did in Idaho—now, that was an outright lie. That one was mine. Bundy must've figured, once he's locked up, he takes credit for the kill, nobody's exactly gonna *volunteer* to come forward, say he's lying.

"That's how *I* figured out what I needed. Just in case, I mean. I needed some sorta way to tell everyone where I been, in case I ever had to *prove* it. And I guess now's the time.

"The way it started, the idea, I mean, was because I done a lot of hunting when I was a kid. So what I decided, I'd just skin 'em when I was done with 'em. And that's what I done down in the Canyon."

Off-camera: "Are those the first ones you did like that?"

"Not even close," the speaker scoffed. "There's quite a few others, scattered here and there. When you find them, you'll always find my brand on them, too."

Off-camera: "Where would we find them, Mark?"

"Mark? I call *you* by your first name? I don't feel like talking anymore. Take me back to my house."

The screen flickered to black.

"Anything?" the blond man asked.

The consultant looked around the room. He took off his

glasses, rubbed them on the lapel of his muted green sports coat, and said: "He's not the one you want."

"What?! " Percy half-snarled.

"It's not him. He had nothing to do with the Canyon Killings. He's just dancing, playing a game, bargaining with the only cards he has left. Towers is a psychopath, all right, but he's not your man."

"What *is* a psychopath, Doc?" Tiger asked, leaning forward, interested for the first time. "Everybody throws that word around, but they never say what it means."

The consultant turned slightly to meet the Amazon's eyes: "Psychopath, as in 'pathology.' They're not 'crazy' in any clinical sense, but they're always missing a few pieces from normal. Like morality . . . or what we call morality, anyway. Some are fearless, some are cowards. But this much is a guarantee: they *all* lack a conscience of any kind, they *all* share a profound sense of entitlement, and *none* possess the quality of basic human empathy.

"But that's where the generalizations end. Actually, many of them are what we call 'ambulatory'—they walk among us and we never see them. But no matter how they come across, they're all very straight-line in their thinking. Personal-need gratification drives all of them. The reason that some fly under the radar is that different psychopaths seek different gratifications."

"Come on, Doc," Tiger urged him, knowing there *had* to be more.

"I understand you're looking for a common factor, some way to link a series of killings. But the only thing all psychopaths have in common is their deficiencies. What makes them different is not what they have, it's what they lack. They never *feel* much of anything. You won't find any trace of remorse, anxiety, depression, and so on. Many of them have learned to fake such feelings to a remarkable extent.

This would be especially true of malingerers—people who have something to gain by appearing to suffer from a mental illness. And, actually, very common among those who've been in 'treatment programs' while incarcerated."

"Roger that," Percy said.

"Some psychopaths are intellectually gifted," the consultant continued. "And some are downright stupid. But they're *all* dangerous, every single one of them.

"Think of them as Outsiders. I don't mean 'outlaws,' I mean outside the human race. This guy on the screen is pure toxic waste, no question. But he's *not* the answer to your question."

"Didn't you write an article for the *Journal of Forensic Psychiatry?* 'Trophy Taking as a Subset of Serial Killer Typology'?" Wanda asked, slyly.

The consultant threw her a half-salute, acknowledging that she'd done her homework. "I sure did, ma'am. But this boy—the one on your screen over there—he's no trophy-taker. He's a sadistic rapist, and he's a killer, no question. But there's another ingredient common to all psychopaths that we haven't talked about yet—they're all capable of lying so plausibly that they fool even the most experienced interrogators."

"Like to see one of them pass a polygraph," Percy muttered.

"Like to see one of them *not*," the consultant retorted. "A polygraph measures heartbeat, blood pressure, galvanic skin response—all indicators of self-perceived guilt. Most of us feel guilty when we lie—and control questions can usually deal with the natural anxiety *anyone* would feel hooked up to the machines. But a psychopath doesn't know what guilt is—they never even bounce the needles on those machines."

Percy didn't respond. But his darkening complexion spoke volumes.

The consultant waited to see if there were any further challenges. Hearing none, he continued: "This Towers individual doesn't present any diagnostic difficulties. He kills when he panics, and he panics every time one of his sexual assaults doesn't go according to his script. I don't know any more than what you already told me, plus the material you sent, but I guarantee you that when they search his lousy little furnished room, or the car he was living out of, they won't find any women's panties, or hair ribbons, or Polaroid photos . . . nothing like that.

"Why? Because, in his mind, the women he raped all wanted him. That's the music playing in his head, and there's only one tune on that jukebox. Mostly rapes, but some homicides. The only women who *didn't* want him are the ones he killed. To him, those women would be 'cock-teasers.' Miserable lying sluts who led him on, then pulled back at the last minute.

"But they were *not* trophies, nor was the style of killing designed to 'pose' the victims. He already knows how long any death-penalty appeal is going to take, and he still wants to do everything possible to extend that time. What he *really* wants is to be extradited. The state where the Canyon Killings took place didn't have the death penalty at the time they occurred. They were still in what we call the *Furman* window, when the Supreme Court struck down the death penalty on constitutional grounds. All of the death-penalty states had to rewrite their laws to comply with that ruling, but they couldn't do it retroactively. Why do you think Manson still gets parole hearings?

"So what this Towers individual is doing is working this unsolved case the same way any good psychopath would—he's *using* it. The more he pulls a Henry Lee Lucas blanket over law enforcement's eyes, the better treatment he gets. Soon, he'll be getting deranged women to write him love letters . . . and *those* he'll want to keep. He'll probably negotiate a book-and-movie deal, too.

"But, like I said, not all psychopaths are intelligent. This one blew it on the time line. The Canyon Killings were more than forty years ago. He probably read about them in one of those 'true crime' porno books. But you've got a verified DOB on this beauty—pretty hard to kill before you've even been born."

"Look," the blond man said, "let's say we already knew all that. And we have plenty of reasons—solid forensic reasons—to take this freak out of the picture on the Canyon Killings. That's not the real reason we brought you here."

"I figured as much," the consultant said, unfazed. "Point out the target and I'll take my best shot."

"Is there anything you can tell us? Anything about who *would* do the kind of thing we've been studying?"

"Whoever did the Canyon Killings, now, *there's* your trophy-taker. Classic 'collector' mentality."

"Some psychopaths take trophies, and *this* one took human spinal cords?" Tiger said, a slight trace of disbelief in her tone.

"I don't think so," Doc answered. "It doesn't feel like that to me. I don't get that same sense of triggering—where something sets them off *after* a killing. It feels more as if whoever did these thought removing the skin of the victims would reveal whatever was under it.

"And don't even say 'organized serial killer' to me. The Canyon Killings actually come across almost like . . . like an investigation of some kind."

"What's this 'investigation,' then?" the tiger-maned woman demanded. "Isn't that what you're here to tell us?"

"Yeah," Percy echoed. "Isn't that what makes you worth seven hundred bucks a damn hour?"

The husky man again rubbed his glasses, this time with a

pristine handkerchief. "You think my services aren't worth what I charge, don't hire me next time."

"We didn't—"

"That's right. *You* didn't hire me. The people who did, *they're* smart enough to listen to what they paid for."

"What are you saying?" Wanda asked, using a tone indicating that she really wanted to know.

"I'm saying that there has to have been more of those killings, and all with a connector of some kind. Like one of those video games where there could be a thousand playing at any one time, all over the world. That's the part nobody's been listening to. Up till now, I'm thinking."

"But doesn't that fit? He couldn't have done the Canyon Killings. And he had to know we know. In fact, didn't you actually *say* that doing that interview was just a game to him?"

"There's more than one kind of game," the consultant answered. "The part where you blew it was not asking enough questions."

"What questions?" the blond man asked, as close to angry as he ever allowed himself to get.

"Questions such as why would they put together a team like *you* folks for signature killings that happened such a long time ago? You're not exactly the Cold Case Squad. So I'm thinking that this *is* about the Canyon Killings, but that those aren't even close to being the only ones. Like I said, the kind of game I'm trying to tell you about, it's a game where there's got to be more than one player."

"You mean the killer had—?"

"Try *listening* instead of showing me you know stuff," the consultant cut off whatever the blond man had wanted to say. "I don't mean some little 'team,' like the Hillside Stranglers, or another *folie à deux* creature like Bernardo-Homolka. Not even Nietzsche-freaks like Leopold-Loeb. I mean a game where the players don't even know each other. But it's a game where they sure as hell keep score.

"And please *don't* start babbling about some cyber-nonsense. That's just the plot of a bad novel. However the players in *this* game are keeping score, they had a way to share info centuries before anyone could *spell* 'Internet.'"

♣

A MAN some know as "Cross" scaled a back-alley fence as calmly as another man would climb a flight of stairs, then gingerly began to lower himself over the far side. Halfway down, he heard the low, menacing growl of a dog he had no desire to meet. Retreating immediately, he then skirted the area, carefully circling past the dog's continuing threats.

He's really worked up. Sensing I'm close. So why didn't he attack as soon as I stepped over the fence? The question had to be answered, so Cross quickly extracted a night-vison monocular. One glance showed him that the dog—from its size and shape, a Rottweiler—was heavily chained, with sufficient play in the heavy links to allow him to protect *one* house against intruders.

Cross nodded his understanding—this was a neighborhood where the only time you'd be concerned about your neighbors was if one of them decided to pay you a visit. He turned his attention to his objective—the back of a six-story tenement.

Chicago is a city of alleys, and it didn't take him much time to find a new approach. A quick, light jump and Cross had the bottom of the fire escape in both hands. He pulled himself up to the first floor, then moved noiselessly upward, his expression that of a commuter on his way to a boring job.

Mentally counting the stories, he located the specific window he was looking for, breathed deeply, exhaled, and waited. After a full minute passed without incident, Cross pulled a roll of duct tape from his voluminous black coat.

He applied the tape to the window glass, smoothly creating an X-pattern until the entire pane was coated. After another careful aural scan, Cross smacked the glass with the palm of his black-gloved hand. The faint crackling sound was barely audible.

Cross picked at the tape-covered glass with his fingertips for a long minute, then carefully peeled it away in a single sheet, leaving only some small shards at the edges of the window. He gently placed the taped glass pane on the fire-escape ledge, then used an L-shaped steel bar to remove the remaining shards from the window. Those he placed on the taped glass pane. Then he stepped through the opened window.

Although the outside of the building appeared to be a landlord-neglected slum, the interior of the particular apartment Cross entered was luxurious. He pulled out a blue-light flash and slowly scanned the premises. The floors were all coated in white shag, the walls covered with "art" chosen to proclaim its cost.

Patiently, Cross moved from room to room. Within minutes he found what he'd been looking for—an electronic scale on a raised marble slab, standing like an idol on an altar.

Cross took a small, flat device from his pocket, held it against the marble base, and pushed a button. A faint light began to appear. The device was soundless, but the intensity of its light glowed in proportion to how close Cross got to his goal—a small safe set into the floor in one corner. On its face was an inset panel with an elaborate set of digital readouts: J6528815.

Cross pulled a slip of paper from an inside pocket, and read it with the aid of his flash: X7324545.

He was leaning forward to tap the digital dial when he heard a low meow and saw its source was a magnificent seal-point Siamese. The feline made another noise deep in its throat, continuing its fearless approach. Cross picked up the cat and stroked its fur, noting that it had been declawed to preserve the furnishings, reducing it to nothing more than another visible sign of wealth.

"You don't give a damn if I empty the joint out, do you, pal?" he said, very softly. Then he set the cat down and tapped the digital dial in accordance with the code on the paper he'd brought with him. The safe popped open. It was almost completely stuffed with cash, but a separate-slotted compartment held a thin red leather book.

Cross didn't touch the money. He took an exact replica of the book from his coat, exchanged it for the original, and closed the safe. Then he tapped the code in reverse, which returned the dial to its original number.

Next, he covered the top and front of the safe with a thick foam pad, then slammed a small sledge over it several times. When he removed the foam, the safe looked as if some amateur had tried to hammer off the dial.

Cross performed a smash-and-grab on a few small objects in the living room, snatched loose cash from a bedroom chest of drawers, and slid an iPhone and its attached Bose headset into another pocket of his coat.

Just another half-ass junkie burglar, he thought to himself as he retraced his steps to the window.

The cat watched, mildly interested.

Cross turned and watched the cat, obviously making some sort of decision.

After a long minute, he shrugged his shoulders and left. His exit was as silent as his entrance. And as unobserved.

♣

CROSS SAT in a stark, cement-walled room. Furnished in minimalist fashion, it was, nevertheless, comfortable, with everything that might be expected in an expensive apartment. Except windows.

In his hands, he held the thin red book he had liberated from the drug lord's safe, studying its construction intently.

Finally satisfied, he delicately removed the backing from a strip of paper that exactly matched the inside back cover of the book. He then laid the strip parallel to the book's binding, pressed it down with a latex-gloved thumb, and used a surgeon's scalpel to trim the top and bottom. Even under an intense light, the new addition was undetectable.

Cross pocketed a transmitter small enough to fit inside a pack of cigarettes. He picked up a cell phone, tapped in a number, and patiently let it ring until it was answered with an aggressive "*¿Qué?*"

"*Finito*," Cross said, just before he cut the connection.

♣

THE NEXT night.

Cross merged his body with the shadows as he waited against the wall of a gas station. Long ago abandoned, the cement building was now an outpost on an urban prairie, surrounded by flatlands peppered with scraps of old cyclone fence. Rusted concertina wire trailed on the ground, derelict cars dotted the deserted street, half-starved dogs skulked in unconscious imitation of the rats they were reduced to hunting.

A black stretch limo pulled up. An over-muscled, blank-faced man with a distinctly small head climbed out of the front passenger seat. He stood by the door, arms crossed over his chest, pumping himself up. After so many years, those movements were pure habit.

Cross stepped out of the shadows.

The window in the back compartment of the limo descended. A cancerous voice floated out: "You have it?"

"Like I said," was the only reply.

The extra-wide back door swung open, a clear invitation. Cross entered, unaware that a tiny black blob had followed him. The blob was unseen by the bodyguard, who continued his posing before the mirror that was always in his mind.

The only human occupant of the back seat was a toadish little creature. He held out a severely mangled hand, with clawed, yellowish nails. Cross dropped the book into his palm.

The toadish man immediately began skimming through the book, following the entries with a skeletal finger.

"*¡Verdad!* The real thing. *¡Dios mío!* You are as good as they say."

Cross reacted to the praise with a question he has asked many others, many times.

"*¿Dónde está mi dinero?*"

"Huh! *¿Sabes español?*"

"*Suficiente para esto.*"

"*¿Esto?*"

"*Mi dinero,*" Cross repeated, making it clear that his language skills were limited to his sole area of interest.

"*¿Su dinero?* Right here, *amigo*. Money, it means nothing. Here," he said, handing over a slim aluminum attaché case, "count it for yourself. What I have purchased from you tonight is so much more precious. By next week, I will control all of Esteban's territory."

Disdaining any gesture of respect, Cross took the toadish man up on his offer to count the money, quickly but carefully.

As Cross counted, the toadish man said, "You know, *amigo*, I like you. I thought that little bit of unhappiness down south could become . . . perhaps a problem between us? But now I see you understand how the world truly works. That was only business then. And this is business now. What else matters?"

Cross shrugged his shoulders, as if the statement was beyond debate.

"You are a true professional," the cancerous voice said. "Revenge, that is for amateurs. Children who may never grow up to learn the reality of life. We are a dying breed, you and I. Dinosaurs. It is good we can still do business with each other. Now, while there are some of us still alive."

He offered his mangled hand. Cross grasped it, the bull's-eye tattoo on the back of his own hand clearly visible. Without another word, he stepped out of the limo, the attaché case in that same hand.

As he did so, a blotchy mass coalesced across the top of the abandoned gas station, disturbing only the molecules of air it displaced.

"Dying breed," bubbled from the shadowy blob.

Five seconds of silence followed. Then:

"Me da una tarjeta de."

As the limo rounded the next corner, the blotchy mass flowed down the side of the gas station. It was still moving when Cross, unaware of any other presence, took the transmitter from his coat pocket and pressed its single button.

The limo disappeared in a blast that looked low-yield nuclear in the fireball of its intensity. All that remained was a crater in the empty street. A few scraps of human flesh mingled with metallic flakes as they floated gently to the ground.

By then, Cross was already several blocks away, behind the wheel of one of the "abandoned" cars. He drove for another couple of minutes, re-"abandoned" the car, and disappeared into the dark.

He never saw the two playing cards floating down to the

crater left by the annihilated limousine. Or the total disappearance of the shadow that had followed him inside the limo.

The floating cards were a suited pair: the ace and jack of spades.

♣

CROSS DIDN'T go far. Against the back wall of a wood-planked, sawdust-floored bar, he walked over to a pay phone with an "Out of Order" sign plastered over the dial.

Standing with his back against the wall, he picked up the receiver, waited a few seconds for a series of clicks, then said, "It's done," into the mouthpiece.

Then he departed as unobtrusively as he entered, as visible to the patrons as a gentle breeze to an elephant.

♣

A SUBTERRANEAN poolroom was buried somewhere in the lower depths of the city. The building was not on any postal route, and the surrounding area had never been assigned a ZIP code. All of that property had been claimed by the city under "Eminent Domain," and was marked on a planning map as a potential bypass to a nearby thruway.

It would retain that status forever. In Chicago, politicians expect to be paid to "expedite" such projects, and not a dime had come their way since a developer had paid for the conversion to "Eminent Domain" status. That developer had conducted all his business over the phone, including the wire transfers. And had made no contact since.

A sloppily sprayed red "71" on the side of the concrete-block structure might look like gang graffiti to a tourist. But there are no tourists in this part of town. On the far side of the "71" a red arrow pointed down, like the blood trail of a cape buffalo recently shot by a hunter.

No experienced hunter would follow such a trail. The cape buffalo is the only animal which, when wounded, travels only a short distance . . . then turns and waits.

To reach the building, it was necessary to traverse a vacant lot littered with abandoned machinery of every kind, from refrigerators to flatbed tow trucks. Concertina wire was strung randomly about, as if whoever had been setting it in place had lost interest at some point. Various dogs roamed at will. So did feral cats—the two natural enemies seemed to have reached a détente of some kind.

There was no door at the outside of the building, just the red arrow leading to a dark, twisting flight of stairs.

In Chicago, many things are whispered about the joint known as Red 71, but the only one that never changes is the street soldier's credo: "If you don't know, you best not go."

The owner of the apparently empty building was a corporation. Its officers had consistently refused all offers to sell during a prior real-estate boom. Word on the street was that the corporation had outsmarted itself, holding out for a bigger price during the long-since-gone "flip this house" mania.

Another developer had razed the other buildings, cleared the land for new construction . . . and promptly gone bankrupt. Now the sole remaining building was worthless, surrounded by a huge lot choked with refuse and debris, with only the occasional weed poking its way toward the sun. It had been enclosed with a chain-link fence during its construction, but now that fence guarded nothing but garbage, and kept nothing from leaving—the dangerous dogs who ranged free inside its walls were clearly there by their own choice.

The poolroom in the basement was the building's only declared source of income, and that barely netted enough to pay the taxes . . . which it did, religiously.

"We have to own our base," Cross had told the crew years ago. "Own it legit. That's the only way we can protect every square inch." The entire crew had chipped in to make the buy, but, on paper, Buddha owned the whole thing via a closely-held corporation.

Buddha was the only one with an above-ground identity, complete with an address in the suburbs and employment as a limo driver. He filed a tax return every year. Even collected a 20-percent disability pension from the VA, although it was paid to an individual who used another name. As per the corporate governance documents, half the building would go to his wife when he died. The other half would go to the children of a man known only as "Ace"—those two were the only crew members with "heirs" of any kind.

The poolroom was actually a subbasement. It stood at the foot of a winding stone staircase, and contained manicured green felt tables, spaced around the floor at a good distance from each other. Two corners of the room also featured small, round tables and empty chairs.

Although some of the inhabitants were shooting pool, others used the felt surface as a dice table, or played cards standing up. Red 71 guaranteed the safety and privacy of all who entered for the transaction of outlaw business, from dealing contraband to putting out contracts. That guarantee no longer had to be demonstrably enforced. Word had long since conveyed the message that those who entered with a wrong idea of what awaited were never going to leave.

The crowd was multi-ethnic, but there was no sense of rigid barriers, and the atmosphere was as non-violent as a Martin Luther King vision. No one entering the poolroom was searched for weapons—that would be equivalent to searching a street whore for condoms.

Nor were there signs saying ACT STUPID AT YOUR OWN RISK—they would be superfluous.

Red 71 was always kept well maintained, and usually stayed quiet. The similarity to a graveyard was too obvious to ignore.

There was a fee for this atmosphere, payable to the elderly man who sat behind a flip-up steel counter, with a green eye-shade covering most of his face.

The elderly man might be anyone at any given time. Looking too closely would be as absurd as asking him to make change. Or conversation.

Cross was seated at one of the side tables, talking to a young woman whose back was to the room. He was positioned so that the two men seated to his right and left were between him and anyone who might approach. Even though completely unnecessary inside Red 71, the positioning was a habitual characteristic of this ultra-pragmatic man-for-hire.

Cross, to quote a man who once did business with him, "don't look like much," but his economy of movement and hyper-vigilance marked him as a survival expert. There was a thick yellow lightning-bolt scar on his right hand, impossible to ignore. That hand held a smoldering cigarette. The woman was hunched forward, whispering urgently, studiously ignored by everyone present.

Two young Chinese were playing a game of nine-ball in one corner. They dressed in traditional Hong Kong gangster style: black leather jackets over neon shirts, the top buttons opened to better display their gold-chain collections. Their hair was long and slicked straight back. As one chalked his cue, the other stepped close and whispered, "You sure that's him?"

"It's him, all right. Just like Chang said. That scar on his hand, it's like a brand—can't miss it."

"Yeah? Well, I *still* don't like this much. All of a sudden, we got some weird-ass white man in a cheap suit for a boss?"

"That man ain't our boss, man. It was *Chang* who told us what to do, not him. *That's* our job, do what Chang tells us."

"I still don't like that bleached-out dude. I don't like nothing about him."

"Why tell me? You don't want to do what some albino says, you know who you got to tell that to. Now go make a call, okay? Don't matter to me *who* you dial. But if it's not that blond guy, you on your own from then on out, brother."

Thus chastised, the young Chinese moved away, walking toward a bank of pay phones against one wall.

♣

INSIDE THE War Room, the blond man picked up a telephone and listened intently, his face a mask of concentration. When the speaker was finished, the blond man said, "Tell Chang, if this information was good, we're all square. He'll understand."

The blond hung up and immediately barked, "We got a locate! Basement poolroom—the one they call 'Red 71.' Get a team out there. Go!"

"I don't see why we can't just bring him in," Percy said. "I'll bet I could make him a better listener."

"We don't have that much data on him," the blond replied, "but what we have indicates we'll need a different approach if we want him to sign on."

"You spooks are all the same. 'Data,' my ass. He's nothing but another mercenary, this Cross guy, right? If leaning on him don't do the job, money will. One or the other always does."

He didn't notice Wanda sadly shaking her head as she caught the blond man's eye. "Show him," she said.

"Show me what?" Percy demanded.

"The 'data,'" Wanda answered, smiling evilly.

♣

WANDA THREW a toggle switch and the larger monitor came to life. An apparently abandoned building appeared, its status confirmed by a large sign proclaiming it an URBAN RENEWAL PROJECT.

The camera's eye moved closer. It showed descending steps, then a close-up of a man's hand, rapping a pattern on a steel door.

The door opened. A heavily muscled man with a circled black swastika on one biceps said, "Play or Watch?"

"Play," a man's voice responded.

"No charge, then. Players' section is on the whole far side of the pit. See it?"

"Yeah."

The camera panned to show several rows of unmatched chairs. Some looked more comfortable than others; most were already filled.

The camera turned and looked directly at the door through which it was entering.

"How'd we get all this?" Percy asked.

"Undercover. Packing a fiber-optic multi-cam," Wanda answered, speaking to Percy as one would a child. A slow child.

"That's a dogfighting setup."

"Uh . . . we *see* that," Tiger said, disgust clear in her voice.

"Oh, yeah; I forgot. You're not just a psycho-killer dyke, you're an animal lover, too."

"Not *all* animals," Tiger hissed at Percy, the disgust in her voice now replaced with unmistakable threat.

"Stop!" the blond man demanded. "You all signed on under the same conditions. What you're looking at is the *only* footage we have of our subject, and—"

"I don't see no 'subject' there."

"Try some patience," the blond man advised, wearily. His tone of voice clearly indicated this was not the first time he'd said that. To the same man. With the same results.

Several minutes rolled by as the cameras swept the room. Shown: a betting board with records and odds posted, men negotiating private cash wagers, dog handlers setting out their instruments.

And caged dogs. Some snarling, some in a near-frenzy, some eerily calm. All awaiting their turn in the just-constructed "pit" . . . which was nothing more than a square of piled railroad ties, with a white line spray-painted down its middle.

"What's that?" Tiger asked, pointing to what looked like a thin thread of black slithering across the top of the monitor's screen.

"Probably some little software glitch," Wanda answered. "Not worth tracking down now. Besides, the show is about to start."

The crowd was mostly male, with a few overdressed women, all visible through a faint haze of cigarette and cigar smoke.

A harsh white baby spot hit the center of the pit, illuminating a man wearing a short-sleeved red shirt over dark slacks. He brought a cordless microphone to his mouth and announced . . .

"Ladies and gentlemen, tonight we—"

Suddenly, two men climbed into the pit area. One was white, thoroughly unremarkable in appearance except for a prominent lightning-bolt scar on his right hand; the other was black, with a triangular face defined by high cheekbones. He was immaculately and expensively dressed, his all-black outfit topped with a matching Zorro hat.

A moviegoer might mistake the black man for a pimp, except that, instead of gold around his neck, he wore a *very* sawed-off shotgun on a leather thong.

Before anyone could react to the intrusion, the black man swung the scattergun up and fired both barrels. The headless announcer's body slumped to the floor as the black man calmly broke his shotgun, flicked his wrist to eject both spent shells, and reloaded both barrels using the same hand.

The stunned silence was broken when several men in the audience reached for weapons.

A high-pitched squeak—*"No!"*—momentarily froze those movements as a bunched group of spectators was torn apart by machine-gun fire.

The momentary freeze turned permanent. Some in the audience held their hands away from their bodies in a clear signal of surrender. Others just stared, stunned and immobile.

A large object sailed through the air and landed inside the pit. The camera moved in closer, showing that the object was a human body. Or, more accurately, was *once* a human body.

The unremarkable man picked up the handheld microphone in his right hand and said, "May I have your attention, please?"

If this was his idea of a joke, no trace of it appeared on his face, or in his voice.

"Thank you. Now, please listen carefully. These are your choices: You may get up and leave this place peacefully, or you may stay. Those who choose to stay will not be given a second opportunity to leave. Anyone *not* moving when I stop speaking will never move again."

One of the dog handlers cupped his hands and called out:

"Okay, man. Whatever you say. We're out of here. Just give us a minute to grab up our dogs, okay?"

A red blotch suddenly blooming on the handler's forehead was the answer. Unlike the other gunfire, this kill-shot had been silent.

"Nobody takes *anything*," the unremarkable man said, in the same dry, flat voice.

The black squiggle Tiger had pointed out moved along with the crowd. The multi-cam unit's sound system was not delicate enough to pick up the single word, this time in English:

"Hit."

Everyone still alive stood up. Players and spectators filed out, moving slowly, every hand held open and away from the body it was attached to.

As the camera focused on the exit door, the voice of something close to human roared: "You started it!"

The camera caught only a brief view of what looked like a human leviathan, moving inexorably as it tore through the dog handlers as the dogs would have torn into each other, ripping off body parts as easily as if dismantling cardboard.

The multi-cam only had time to record that the monster's head was shaved, and that he was wearing a banana-colored tank top. Then it went black.

♣

"**WHAT THE** *hell* was—?"

"The man with the microphone, that's the man we want," the blond man said. "His name's Cross. The man next to him is known only as 'Ace.' They've been partners since they came into hardball juvie on the same bus."

" 'Hardball juvie' . . . ?"

"Illinois was the first state to differentiate between juvenile and adult offenders," the blond man addressed his small audience somewhat pedantically. "It was still maintaining that façade at the time those two first met. That was an end-of-the-line stop for both of them—their crimes *should* have put them directly into adult corrections, and it was guaranteed their next ones would. And that there *would* be a next one."

"The shaved-head guy?"

"Believe it or not, his name is 'Princess.' Off-the-charts insane. He dresses and speaks like a *very* gay man. Wears all kinds of makeup, minces his words . . . even flounces around waving his wrists. His delusion is that this will encourage others to attack him. In his deranged mind, he is not permitted to attack unless he can claim the other party 'started it.'"

As he spoke, the blond man pushed a button. A full-body photo of Princess appeared on the screen.

"*That's* him? Damn! Whatever he's carrying in that monster shoulder holster—"

"That's a .600 Nitro Express," Percy snapped out, his voice a mix of anger and awe. "A .600 Nitro Express *pistol*. Only one I've ever heard about, never mind seen. That maniac actually carries a sawed-off, over-under elephant gun? A load like that, it'd snap a man's wrist like a toothpick."

"I'm no firearms expert," Tracker said, deliberately ironic, "but do you have any idea why he would carry such a weapon?"

"It goes with his outfit," Tiger half-giggled. "*Très chic, non?*"

Seeing Percy about to respond, the blond man cut him off with the universal "Halt!" signal, then said, "Three hundred and thirty pounds is our best guesstimate of his weight. All of it muscle."

"Why guesstimate?" Wanda asked.

"He's never been in custody," the blond man answered.

"We have various records on the others, but even those are spotty, if not outright fallacious.

"The machine-gunner—he was not shown on camera—is called 'Rhino.' Originally sentenced to an institution for the severely retarded, he was repeatedly tortured until he became—literally—anaesthetic to pain. That's when they went to the Thorazine handcuffs. By the time Cross and Ace were sentenced, he had already been in that same institution for a couple of years."

"But you said he was retarded."

"That's what it said on the first admission papers, Wanda. But he wasn't too retarded to assault staff every time the drugs wore off, so . . ."

"So they locked him in that prison even though he never committed a crime?"

"That *is* what happened, Tiger. It's not our job to judge."

"Oh, really?"

"Yes! Besides, that was *years* ago. What we do know is that this Cross individual—remember, he was just a kid himself at the time—figured out a way to detox the monster. But nobody knew this until Cross—again, I am speaking literally—actually sawed through cell window bars with nothing but dental floss which had been braided, coated with glue, and then rolled in drain-cleaner crystals. It must have taken months of backbreaking work.

"Then this 'Rhino' *bent* the bars, enabling Cross and Ace to escape. It was the belief of staff that Cross, a diagnosed sociopath, had simply used Rhino to achieve his own ends. However, *somebody* later broke him out of custody. No agency has gotten their hands on that monster since."

"Monster?" Tiger persisted.

"See for yourself," the blond man responded, flashing another photo on the monitor. "He's almost seven feet tall and weighs nearly five hundred pounds. Again, those are only estimates—we don't know his actual age, so we can't know if he continued to grow after he escaped.

"By 'monster,' I was referring only to his size, not his disposition. In fact, we don't even know his actual name. The records of his prior institutional 'care' seem to have disappeared."

"I'll just bet," Tiger said. "Okay, that's four men. Four men without one real name among them—is that what you're telling us?"

"Yes."

"Yeah? Well, *someone* took that shot with the silencer."

"Our best guess was that was a man called Buddha. All we know about him is that he and Cross apparently met while serving in what is euphemistically called the 'post-Vietnam' era. His service records don't indicate combat. Or anything else, for that matter. However, Military Intelligence informs us that the man is an expert shot, especially with handguns, a truly gifted driver, and a criminal to his core."

As the blond man spoke, the photo on the monitor showed a slumped-shouldered man with a vaguely Oriental cast to his dark, cold eyes.

"We *do* know his wife is Korean. What she was doing somewhere around the Laos-Cambodian border is anybody's guess. All we have for her is what we assume was a street name: 'So Long Li.' She is, however, reputed to be utterly absorbed in acquiring money, and quite skillful at doing so. Of the entire Cross gang, Buddha is the only one for whom we have an actual address—a freestanding house in the Uptown area. In his wife's name, of course."

"What's wrong with that?"

"Nothing is 'wrong' with that, Tiger. The point was simply to emphasize his wife's obsession with materiality."

"And what's this 'post-Vietnam' designation . . . ?"

"It's the same for *all* of them, Wanda. Apparently, some

sort of bargain was struck between the man we know as 'Cross' and one of the . . . agencies operating in the field at that time. All the records concerning Cross and Buddha have been death-wipe overwritten. How that came to include Ace—who never served in the military—is not information we have."

"Not the first time *that* trick was pulled," Percy said. "Who cares about names, anyway? What I want to know is what that . . . whatever we just saw . . . what was *that* all about?"

"The Cross gang was hired by person or persons unknown to shut down a dogfighting operation," the blond man said, in the bored voice of a Mafia don taking the Fifth for the hundredth time.

"And for that they slaughtered a couple dozen people?" Percy responded, a faint note of admiration seeping into his deep voice.

"That's how he came by his name."

"Huh?"

" 'Cross.' That's not just the name he 'enlisted' under, it's his reputation. He specializes in twofers, understand?"

"Kills the guy who hires him to kill another guy?"

"Nothing that simple, but that's the idea. If he got paid to take out a couple of *individuals* inside that building by one person *and* put the dogfighting operation out of business by another, that would be more consistent with his reputation."

"The cops," Percy asked, "didn't they lean on the others? The ones who walked out, I mean."

"There were no survivors," the blond man said, no trace of surprise in his voice. "The crowd that walked out walked into . . . something. They ended up exactly like the Canyon Killings, every one of them."

"Good," Tiger snarled.

"What are you, PETA on steroids?" Percy cracked.

"Anytime you want to find out—"

"Enough!" the blond man said, using his broken-record voice.

"All this . . . stuff," Wanda complained. "We have names like 'Cross' and 'Buddha' and 'Rhino' and 'Ace' and 'Princess.' That's it? Speaking of which, do we at least have a real name for this 'Princess'?"

"Not even close," the blond man told her. "All we know is that a crew Cross put together did some kind of 'work' in Central America. We don't know who he did it for, but we do know two things: one, he lost a couple of men in that operation, and two, he brought Princess back with him."

"Lost a couple of men?" Tiger mused aloud.

"Yeah, that's another thing about this guy. He's *obsessed* with revenge. You want to see the effects of *real* terrorism, just say his name around any of the local gang leaders. But if we don't know the identities of the men he lost, we can't know if he ever took care of whoever he held responsible."

"That's a good rep to have," Tiger said. "Makes anyone thinking of pulling a fast one think again."

"That's not just his rep," the blond man corrected her, "it's part of a profile we commissioned. Outside his own crew, people are nothing but chess pieces to him. Like I said before, a sociopath."

"Right. And he's *still* with the same men he partnered up with a million years ago?"

"I'm not disagreeing. Any idiot would make that connection. I agree—that single fact contradicts the diagnosis. And we'll confirm that with the doctor when the chance comes. We do know one thing which binds his crew completely. A question anyone who wants to join them has to answer. But it's just a phrase, and we can't translate it."

"Well?" Wanda said, tapping the side of her keyboard with her fingernails to indicate her impatience.

"Here it is: 'Do you hate them? Do you hate them *all*?'"

"Who's 'them'?"

"There are hundreds of pages of guesses. But that's all they are—guesses."

"Bunch of psychos," Percy dismissed the "info" with his usual gift for analysis.

"Could be," the blond agreed. "But our Mr. Cross has got one thing going for him that has always worked as a convincer."

"Which is . . . ?"

"He doesn't care if he lives or dies. And it seems as though everybody in this city's underground knows it."

♣

THE MAN called Cross got up and walked through a beaded curtain made up of ball bearings. He entered a back room, three other men behind him. His handprint unlocked a thick door. A blinking orange light alerted him that calls had been made from the pay phones in the poolroom since the system had last been checked.

Buddha tapped the "playback" key. He closed his eyes to concentrate on the tape.

Less than a minute later, he said: "It's what we thought, boss. Reporting to Chang. Only surprise was the guy speaking Mandarin. You'd think Cantonese, coming from those boys. Must be Hong Kong, not mainland."

"You know what to do," Cross said.

Buddha pulled a throw-away cell phone from his field jacket, punched in a number, and had a brief conversation in a language none of the others understood.

"I just told the gray-tooth headman that Chang was working for the *federales*, boss. He said to tell you his 'gratitude' was on its way."

"Chang was going, anyway. Bringing in those MS-13 boys was a mistake. Thinking he could control them, that made it a fatal one."

"You got that right," Buddha agreed. "That MS-13 crew's crazy enough to do any damn thing, but crazy don't beat crafty, and those Cambos are some *seriously* evil plotters."

"They had to be."

"To stay alive when Pol Pot was running that slaughterhouse? Amen to that."

"Yeah," Cross said, without much interest. "Time for me to move out, get this rolling."

♣

AS THE others were re-entering the poolroom, Cross climbed a flight of stairs taking him out of the basement, opened a back door, and exited into the street.

Twenty steps later, he slid into an alley, walking behind an overflowing Dumpster which concealed a metal door. Then he began to climb a long flight of pebble-pocked steel steps.

At the first landing, he pulled out a pocket flash, illuminating a shelf. He took a small bottle off the shelf and sprayed a mist over his right hand. He then took a clean handkerchief and wiped the back of that hand, using only moderate force. The lightning-bolt scar disappeared.

Cross then removed a pre-moistened sheet of fibrous cloth from a slotted box and carefully draped it over his right hand. With his left, he ran a small hair dryer over the sheet for a few seconds. When the sheet was pulled away, the familiar bull's-eye tattoo was back in place.

He then exchanged his leather jacket and T-shirt for an expensively cut charcoal alpaca suit, complete with a stylishly retro fedora. The same alligator boots he had worn when speaking with the woman in the poolroom remained in place. Almost as an afterthought, he spit out the wads of spirit gum that had deformed his facial features while he had been inside the poolroom.

A quick glance in the polished-metal mirror satisfied him. He then resumed his climb.

♣

CROSS STEPPED out onto the rooftop, stopped to check a connected series of wooden boxes with an exit trap and air holes cut for entry-exit, noting it was empty. He didn't bother to add seed to the empty bins—if the mated pair of kestrels were both out, they weren't on a pleasure cruise. But he did refill the water trough, using bottled spring water.

By the time he returned to the alley, a big sedan was waiting.

"You know" was all Cross said to Buddha.

♣

THE CITY-CAMO car moved slowly through an alley. When it came to a full stop, Cross jumped out.

The back staircase of an anonymous building took Cross all the way to the roof. There, he draped a wood plank across the gap to move to the next building. When he reached the other side, he elevated the plank before shoving it effortlessly back across. The Teflon-coated edges of both rooftops had been tested and retested a hundred times. The only difficulty encountered had come when Princess demanded a turn. Rhino protested, Buddha encouraged him. Cross settled it: "If it'll hold his weight, it'll hold mine, right?"

The new building's roof housed an electrical shack. Cross stepped inside. He moved down a flight of stairs to a hallway, where he rang for an elevator marked "Freight."

The elevator car came up, driven by a short, squat Hispanic with a Zapata mustache. Cross got on. The car descended all the way to the basement. Both men got out. The Hispanic looked through a periscope device for a long minute.

"Clear," he told Cross.

Cross stepped around the other man, exchanged a fist-pound for the other's *"Viva la Raza!"*; the man's cynical expression as he pocketed the tightly rolled bills clearly demonstrated that the political-solidarity verbiage had been pure sarcasm.

Neither man was as unseen as either of them believed. Inside what looked like an oversized van sat the blond man and another individual, the latter wearing a white lab coat and trifocal glasses.

The blond man was seated in a captain's chair in the rear, watching the other one peer at a console.

"You got him?" the blond asked.

"Locked on. No place he can go now. He can change his clothes, but he can't change his thermal image. Look. . . ." One of the round monitors flickered. On the screen, the image was the fluid outline of a man, with different areas of his body marked in different colors.

"Is this what . . . *they* . . . use?" the blond asked.

"Far as we can tell, yes. They've got some form of heat-seeker, that's for sure. But it can differentiate better than anything we've ever seen. The technology was so superior that we don't have anything to compare it to. Are you following me?"

"I believe. . . ."

"Just in case you're not, I'll spell it out: they can see us, but we can't see . . . whatever they are. Which is about as bad as it gets. But we've just added something to *our* bag of tricks. With these new instruments, we can pick up *when* they're watching."

"Watching us, you mean?"

"No," the white-coated man said. "We're nowhere near that stage. We can pick up a signal that says their system is activated, but that's *all* we can do. We don't know *who* it's locked on to, just *when* it's gone operational. And then only when it's within our sweep area."

Tiger moved just enough to announce her presence. She nodded in a gesture the blond man understood all too well: unlike Percy, Tiger relied on more than just her eyesight. But her basic premise was the same—if she could sense it, she could kill it.

♣

AS THE team reassembled in the War Room, they continued to track Cross making his way through the underground network of the city: from abandoned tunnels to subbasements of office buildings and finally to an apparently empty shack standing at the end of a shipping pier. The pier itself hadn't been used in years—Cross carefully picked his way across the rotting timbers.

"You know what I can't understand?" the blond man said to Wanda, forcing her to look up from a thick sheaf of computer printouts she had in her lap.

"What is it *this* time?" Wanda responded, her voice tinted with the waspish superiority she could not always restrain.

The blond ignored her attitude—human emotions were of no great interest to him.

"We've got locates on them all over the world. Whatever the hell they are, they don't give a damn about climate."

"So?"

"So look at this pattern. We have a series of kills near the Arctic Circle. Polar-bear hunters. Poachers, as it turns out. Same in Kenya."

"Polar bears in Kenya?" Tiger asked, just short of giggling. "*That's* your pattern?"

"*Poachers*, you stupid slut. In Kenya, they were after rhino horn."

Tiger leaned forward, one fist clenched, her thumb pressing down on the topmost finger. She felt the light touch of the Indian's hand on her arm. Tracker shook his head—not an order, one comrade cautioning another that the time to strike had not yet arrived. Tiger nodded, unclenched her fist, and sat back, crossing her long legs.

"And in Brazil," the blond continued, oblivious to how close he had just come to serious injury, "the same damn thing, only *this* time the victims had been chasing some kind of rare parrot."

Sensing he finally had everyone's attention, the blond looked up. "I know. That's the first thing we thought, some band of crazed environmentalists. Especially with the last one. I mean, it was in their sacred damn rain forest—that's holy ground to those twits."

The monitor showed a forensics team working over the ground in the jungle. Torn and gutted corpses were hanging from nearby trees—all missing some portion of their skeletons.

"But we found one thing in all those kills that eliminated our Green friends. . . ."

As if sync'ed to the blond's words, the monitor zoomed in on what looked like a bloody pelt. This one wasn't hanging, it was carelessly tossed to one side. But it was just as dead.

"Dogs," the blond continued. "Huskies up north, Ridgebacks in Africa, and some kind of mongrel we'd never heard of in South America. All dead. No way the Greenies would kill dogs. Especially like this. They look like they've been clawed into pieces by some ferocious giant cat."

The Indian was lost in thought, concentrating on the data, reaching inside himself for information he knew was in there . . . somewhere.

♣

"**THERMAL'S GREAT** for tracking," the blond man said, three hours later. "But it's not like we can show the footage to a lip-reader."

"Try *watching*," Tiger said. "You see that old Chinese man sitting opposite him now? You think this 'Cross' guy speaks Chinese?"

"In the field, to speak a language you are not expected to know is to discard a potent weapon," Tracker added, supporting the one person on the team he regarded as an equal. "Their talk will all be in English."

All eyes moved to the screen. The Chinese man was wearing some sort of heavily embroidered robe.

"Red," Tracker said. "The color for gold."

"Ssssh," the blond man commanded.

Tiger and Tracker exchanged looks, but said nothing.

If their lip-reader was sufficiently skilled, the team would soon receive the following printout:

"*The Japanese have short memories," the Chinese man said.*

"*I don't."*

"*Yes. This well known, Mr. Cross."*

"*Spare me the tea ceremony, Chang. There's someone missing from this meeting."*

"*And that would be—?"*

"*Mr. Green."*

"Ah. But that gentleman doesn't know the cost of transportation to this place. Not yet."

"Just spell it out. Then I'll tell you what it costs."

"The Japanese are our best market, by far. They will outbid anyone, and they will buy—"

"Yeah. Sure. Fine. Right. Okay."

"I do not understand."

"Then try this: I'm not getting paid to listen to parables. Get down to it. Now. Or I'm gone."

Chang instantly comprehended that the circular negotiation tactics he had been taught since childhood would be futile with the empty-eyed man sitting across from him.

"On the Kamchatka Peninsula live the largest bears in the world. Their paws are worth a fortune—the Japanese will pay whatever is asked. The chain was simple enough to establish. The Russians have a man here in Chicago. His name is—"

"Viktor."

"You do know him. This is most excellent. Viktor is a very greedy individual. We have great hopes that his successor will be more reasonable."

"I like your robe, Chang. Very colorful. Powerful color. This insect that disturbs you? I could probably crush it under that robe of yours with only, perhaps, a twenty-pound weight."

"That is—"

"Troy weight. Half on the table, right now. I take it and go. You won't see me again until I come to collect the second payment."

"That is a great deal of trust you ask, Mr. Cross."

"You called. I came. You asked a price. I gave you one."

"Still, there is always room for reasonable men to discuss such things, is there not?"

"I'm not a reasonable man, Chang. Only two choices on the menu today. And 'maybe' isn't one of them."

♣

THE WINDOW of the large storefront was crudely painted over in a sun-faded shade of red. The only indication of its contents was a black-lettered sign:

Вход открыт только для настоящих преступников!

Cross entered without knocking. The back wall was quite close to the window, indicating the storefront had been divided so that the majority of its space was behind that wall.

There was a single round table to the right, all but one of the eight chairs occupied. Cross took the empty chair.

Across from him, a square-faced, block-jawed man sat. He was missing most of one ear, his nose had been broken so many times that it was snouted into a blob with nostrils, and what appeared to be a steel ball bearing served as his right eye.

Although a freshly washed empty glass sat to the man's right, he made no attempt to fill it. "Russian vodka is only *real* vodka. All else are weak pretenders: ours is the finest in the world. And—ah, you would say it like 'Imperia'—our Imperia vodka is the best *of* that best. You enter our house unmolested, which means we recognize you as a legitimate criminal. And yet you still refuse to share a drink with your brothers, Cross?"

Cross nodded his head, so slightly that the movement would have been undetectable unless watched for.

"Hah! I am not insulted. Do you know why?"

Cross lit a cigarette.

"You do not drink. So it is not my hospitality you refuse; it is merely that you have a delicate stomach."

Cross did not react. The man across from him translated what he himself had just said into Russian. The other men at the table chuckled—they had dealt with Cross before, and the idea of him having a "delicate stomach" was certainly worth a good laugh.

"Chang wants to buy some bear claws," Cross said.

"And he sends you?"

"He *pays* me."

"Chang is one of the cautious ones. That is why he is such an old man."

Cross shrugged. "What do I tell him, Viktor?"

"Tell him . . . Cross, that tattoo on your hand, it was made in prison, yes?"

Cross nodded.

"What does it mean?"

Cross stared through Viktor, but he did not speak.

"Gah! In my country, you *earn* your marks. You see this?" Viktor rose to his feet and pulled up his sweater, revealing an elaborate devil-horned skull, with a snake slithering out of each empty eyeball. The skull was backed by an X-pattern, and surrounded by a strand of barbed wire. Underneath was printed КАУНАС. "Do you know what this means, Cross?"

"No."

"It means 'authority.' How you say this in America? 'Boss,' maybe? But more important than just boss, boss in prison. Understand?"

"Yes."

"Good. Now you know more than most others do about me. So, that one on your hand . . ."

"It's a bull's-eye. A target."

"This anyone can see. Like the paper circles the police recruits shoot at."

Cross flexed his right hand slightly, then flattened his palm over his heart, as a child would recite the pledge of allegiance. "You see any hits on *this* one?"

Again, the big Russian translated. And, again, his crew joined him in laughter.

"*Now* we can talk as equals, yes? Okay, then. For Chang, because I admire that old man so much, only twenty-five thousand. That buys him *one* of what he wants—we have a virtually unlimited supply. And we are the *only* source."

Cross pushed back his chair.

"You have nothing more to say?" Viktor asked.

"I only got paid to listen," Cross answered. And walked to the door.

♣

AS DARKNESS fell, Viktor was standing in front of his headquarters. Despite the weather, he was wearing a thick coat made of bear fur and a hat of the same material.

"*Bolshe!*" he barked into a satellite phone. He listened to the response, then said, "*Ne vazhno!*" into the mouthpiece, and thumbed off the phone.

He signaled to a group of men standing close by. A line of five identical midnight-blue Audi A8 sedans pulled to the empty curb. As Viktor prepared to enter the back seat of the middle car, the satellite phone in his hand seemed to change color, as if a shroud of shadow had been draped over it. A low sound, outside the human hearing threshold, came, short and sharp:

"убил!"

♣

JUST BEFORE daylight, a Chicago cop stared through the windshield of his cruiser. "Holy Jumping Jesus Christ! I've been on the force since before you were born, kid. And I've never seen anything like . . . that."

Both the retirement-age sergeant and the rookie sitting next to him were staring at bodies draped over a row of identical dark-blue sedans. Each body had been skinned, graphically displaying that all were missing large bones, from femurs to skulls.

Neither cop noticed the city-camo shark as it slipped past the scene. Running without headlights, it looked more like a shifting shadow than a car.

Inside that shark, Buddha said, "Someone got to him first, boss." His gloved hands delicately fingered the thickly padded steering wheel as his eyes checked the instrument display projected on the lower windshield.

"Viktor always was an optimist."

"Huh?"

"He was a HALO jumper," Cross said. "Absolutely positive his chute would open whenever he decided to pull the cord. This time, the ground got there first."

"Chang sees a picture of this, he'll think you worked some magic, getting it done so fast."

"Yeah. So will the Russians."

"*They* paid, too?"

"More than Chang. The Russian Bear is a sacred icon to them. In their eyes, Viktor was looting a national treasure."

"But it had to be some of their own people doing the actual poaching."

"Sure. But that's their problem, at their end. We only got paid to solve the one at ours."

"Comes out perfect, boss. It's like Viktor's number came up, and we *hit* that number at the same time."

"Yeah," Cross said. "Perfect."

"What's wrong?"

"Come on, Buddha. You saw those bodies yourself. All of a sudden we got partners? *Silent* partners?"

♣

THE ROUND screen in the War Room flickered. "What the hell is he up to now? More damn driving around the city?" the blond man muttered, moving a joystick to control the screen images.

With the camera's eyes, the team saw Cross step out of the camo car, which immediately pulled away. They watched as he walked to the back of the shack on the pier, grabbed a pole thick enough for a firehouse, and slid smoothly down until he disappeared from sight.

The pole itself went all the way into the water, but Cross only dropped about halfway down—slowing whenever his boots made contact with the stops jutting out of the pole.

Cross then jumped lightly onto a short landing which had been laboriously constructed under the pier. Within seconds, he was inside his hideout.

The blond man was busy at his private computer, tapping in coordinates, watching the screen for data translation. All of a sudden, his expressionless face lit up:

"Got him! Son of a bitch lives in a goddamn *cell*, can you believe it? Let's see, now. . . ." He continued to work the computer as street maps flashed on his screen, from macro to micro, zeroing in.

"Yes!" the blond man half-shouted in triumph. "The waterfront, not far from where the ore boats come across the lake. Let's get rolling. We're looking for a spot on the north side of Pier 29."

♣

THE INSTANT the team's van began to move, it dropped even the vaguest resemblance to any ordinary vehicle. Its sheer mass of "military" and "futuristic" radiated menace.

Cross stepped out of a stall shower, a towel around his waist. He lit a cigarette, sat down in a sling chair, closed his eyes, and blew smoke at the ceiling. His facial expression resembled an Easter Island statue on Botox.

Wanda was working at her computer, handing each new piece of printed-out information to the blond man, who scanned and tossed the sheets over his shoulder the way a wolf works his way through the carcass of a fresh-killed sheep, seeking the most edible parts.

"He's got communications," Wanda said. "Microwave . . . Using a bounce on the transmitter . . . You have to dial a number. . . . Okay, I have it. It's a pay phone. Pulling up the location now."

The camera showed a narrow doorway with discreet neon lettering running vertically in a window slit next to it. The neon spelled out:

O
R
C
H
I
D

B
L
U
E

The camera moved past a muscular woman at the door, her folded-arms stance saying "bouncer" as clearly as if written across her chest. Orchid Blue turned out to be a high-class gay bar, accommodating same-sex and mixed couples both, with nothing outrageously campy allowed. The camera nosed through the place like a patient bloodhound. It ended up in the back, showing a bank of pay phones next to the restroom.

The last phone had a large "Out of Order" sign prominently placed across its face. Closing in, the camera showed that the receiver itself had been severed from the phone—the coiled metal cord dangled, clearly expressing that there was no point even *trying* to make a call.

"Okay," the blond man said, "back to base. It's time to give this Mr. Cross some idea of who he's dealing with."

♣

INSIDE THE War Room, the blond man could not keep the smirk off his face as he punched in a number on the phone console.

"Orchid Blue . . . what kind of name is that for a nightclub?" he asked, slyly. "Any of you guys ever heard of it?"

Everybody shook their heads except Tiger, who gave him a challenging look . . . which he promptly ignored.

A phone rang inside Cross's cave. It continued to ring as he took three precisely spaced drags on his cigarette.

The blond man did not share his target's calmness. He pounded on the console, muttering, "Pick up the damn phone!" at the image on the screen.

Wanda worked the monitor's dials. The image on the round screen sharpened.

Cross reached out a hand, picked up the receiver. Said: "What?"

"Mr. Cross," the blond man said, "I have a proposition for you."

"Yeah, fine. Meet me at . . ."

"There's no need for that, Mr. Cross. And no time. You either step outside when we tell you or we'll be coming to pay a visit in person."

"Visit me where?"

"Right where you are, right this minute. We're locked in on you. In fact, we can see what you're doing even as we speak."

"Is that right?"

"Mr. Cross, we are aware of your little phone-forwarding system, but you are not dealing with a pack of maladroits this time. You don't believe me? I'll make it simple. Raise your hand; I'll tell you how many fingers you're holding up. Come on, go ahead. . . ."

The screen flickered. Tiger chuckled.

"Very funny, Mr. Cross. And very mature as well. Have I convinced you yet?"

"What is it you want, buddy?"

"I'm not your buddy. And what I want is for you to step out of your cave long enough for a civilized conversation. You listen to our proposition. That's it. Nothing more."

"How close are you?"

"Forty-five minutes."

"I'll be outside."

♣

AS THE surveillance van picked up speed, homing in on its objective, Cross took inventory, as if considering a number of propositions. He glanced at a round hatch-style door set into his back wall—obviously an emergency escape route. The red pull-down handle made it clear that this was an option which could only be used once.

Finally, he shook his head and started to get dressed.

♣

WHEN THE van rounded the last corner, Cross was stand-ing at the edge of the pier, hands in the pockets of a coat that trailed to his ankles, so voluminous it could almost be a wraparound cape. The coat was a distinctive bright white with a high collar and wide raglan sleeves. At his feet, Cross had a small satchel, roughly the size and shape of a doctor's bag. His back was against a wood pylon.

The van pulled to a stop. Man and machine eyed each other, waiting.

The side of the van opened with a hissing noise—a hydraulic panel, not a hinged door. Tracker jumped lightly to the ground and approached Cross, his hands open at his sides. He bowed slightly.

"I am Tracker. Will you come with us?"

Cross returned the bow, perhaps an inch lower, maintain-ing eye contact. "You're not the one who talked to me on the phone."

"That one is inside. Where you should be . . . so that we can explain our offer to you without observation."

"Down here, you don't have to worry about stuff like that. Looking into another man's business could get you killed."

Tracker shifted his body slightly, checking the area, sweeping with his eyes. "The . . . thing we're after, you wouldn't see it coming."

"The thing *you're* after. Not my problem, then."

"It will be, I promise you. Very soon, too. If we meant you harm, you'd be gone now. I have approached you respect-fully, have I not?"

After five seconds of utter stillness, Cross walked toward the van, deliberately allowing the Indian to move in behind him. He walked ponderously, as if his coat was a suit of armor.

Cross climbed inside the van, took the seat gestured by the Indian, and found himself directly across from the blond man.

The blond man smiled his thin smile, asked Cross, "Can I take your coat?"

"No."

"I didn't think so. I assume you won't be offended if I don't offer to shake hands. Our records indicate considerable expertise in improvised weaponry. I'm told you can kill a man with a sharpened credit card."

Cross gave him a contemptuous look. "There's women who can do that with a dull one."

Percy laughed.

Tiger crossed her arms under her heavy breasts, arched her back, and spit out: "Maybe you should try a woman you don't have to pay for. Provided you can find one, that is."

Cross turned to her. "I apologize. I didn't mean to offend you. There's something about this guy I don't like, and I let it make me say something stupid. That's not professional. I was wrong."

Tiger's expression changed, but she watched closely to see if she was being played with. And finally decided she was not. She uncrossed her arms, leaned a bit forward.

"That's okay," she smiled, "I don't like him, either."

The blond man remained profoundly uninterested in all this—he was well accustomed to people not finding him likable.

"Sorry for the demonstration," he told Cross, "but we didn't have time to approach you through the usual channels."

"You want to hire me, then?"

"That's exactly what we want."

"What's the job?"

"If it's all right with you, I'd like to show you rather than tell you. That means a drive to our HQ, but it'll be easier that way. Quicker, too."

Cross shrugged, flashing back to the cold truth of what Tracker had told him: if these people wanted him dead, he'd have stopped breathing some time ago.

But that possibility cut both ways. Now that he had the satchel he carried inside a closed space, he knew his crew was safe, no matter how this ended. If things went wrong, he wouldn't be leaving even a scrap of DNA behind.

"Call it up," the blond said into the microphone.

♣

BACK IN the War Room. Everybody was there, including Percy. He doesn't get out much, unless there's something requiring combat skills. Or kills.

The blond man made the introductions. Nobody shook hands.

"Why him?" Cross asked Tracker, jerking his thumb at the blond man.

"Why not?"

"Because it's personal for you," Cross said. "Not for him."

Wanda didn't speak, just threw a couple of keystrokes at her type pad.

Tracker tapped his heart as the large monitor flashed on an Indian hunting party returning to camp, finding those they left behind hanging upside down, bleeding out, stripped of bone matter.

Cross nodded his understanding.

"Why not ask me, too?" Tiger half-snarled. As if in compliance, Wanda hit more keys.

"They took out three of my sisters," Tiger whispered as the monitor showed three women, all armed to the teeth, standing in a back-to-back-to-back triangle in some sort of tunnel. Their faces reflected both calmness and rage—warriors facing certain death, determined not to go easily. Or alone.

Cross lit a cigarette. Wanda's face showed disapproval. Cross didn't look nervous, didn't look bored, didn't look impatient.

Finally, the blond man broke the silence. "We know what you are, Mr. Cross. And we have a job for you."

"You don't have a clue about what I am, pal. All you know is what I do."

"Meaning . . . ?"

"I don't know what you do, and I don't give a damn. But I know what you *are*."

A grin flashed across Tiger's face. Even Percy nodded his head in agreement.

"We didn't bring you here to play word games," the blond said.

"You don't know me. Maybe you know some of the things I've done. Or I'm supposed to have done. Whatever, you don't know much more than rumors. You don't want to play word games, you can stop talking in code anytime you want. Just get down to it. What do you want done?"

"The job—"

"Not the job, the price. Say the figure for me to get something done. Or the threats if I don't, whatever you deal in."

"Neither. How about you just tell us whether you've ever seen anything like this before?" The blond tossed some photographs on the table in front of Cross.

A number of corpses, hanging upside down as one might hang a slaughtered steer to drain its fluids. The blurred background was a thatched hut of some kind, suggesting only an equatorial climate.

"Yeah," Cross said, bringing a look of surprise to the blond's face.

"Where?" he asked.

"Africa. We came back from patrol, found the whole sweeper team hung up, exactly like that."

"What did you think it was?"

"What did I *think* it was? We all *knew* what it was. A message from the Simbas. That's the way they did things over there: kill your enemy and leave his head on a stake. Discourages anyone else from hanging around."

"Did it work on you?"

"Sure," Cross replied, surprising the blond once again.

"Then look at these. . . ." The blond tossed more pictures on top of the originals. All same-signature corpses, but the settings were vastly different. A penthouse apartment, a hunting lodge, an abandoned warehouse. No individual bodies, all multiple kills.

"They all look alike," Cross said, neglecting to mention that he had viewed an exactly similar scene only a short while ago.

"Those scenes are not—"

"Not the scenes."

"What, then?"

"The bodies of the losers."

"Don't you mean 'victims'?"

"Fighters aren't victims. These are all some kind of battle sites. And a C-note to a dime says it wasn't civilians who got taken out."

"They . . . ?"

"I told you before. The Simbas."

"Wanda . . . ?" The blond man turned to her. She was busily tapping away at the computer keyboard with one hand, clicking a silver pen against her teeth with the other. "Simbas . . . Got it. None ever captured alive. Some of the intel says they're a myth. Not really a tribe at all. There's no hard—"

"A myth?" Tracker interrupted, surprising everyone on the team. "Like the so-called Seminoles in Florida? They set up base in the Everglades, down where Stonewall Jackson wouldn't go after them. So they had to call Cherokees who refused to walk the Trail of Tears by something other than their true name. It was Jackson who named them Seminoles—that way, he could tell the government that all the Cherokees were accounted for. Same as those Vietnam body-counts.

"You know what my favorite song is," Tracker continued, his voice heavy with a dull-thudding backdrop of ancient hate. "It's called 'Cherokee Nation.' Naturally, a bunch of white men got to sing it. Even named themselves after the white man's heroes: 'Paul Revere and The Raiders.'"

"We were here before Columbus," Tracker said, his tone making it clear that he was not inviting a response. "Maybe the Cherokee word for 'blanket' should be 'smallpox,' too."

"That does fit the Simbas," Wanda said, gently breaking into the silence that followed.

"Yeah?" Percy asked. "How's that make any sense?"

"Start from here," Wanda recited, reading from her scrolling screen. "Allegedly, the Simbas are the only known tribe of mixed Africans. . . ."

"Black and white?" Percy asked, now genuinely curious.

"No, *tribal*-mixed. That almost never happens. And, when it does, it's usually a war-rape. But with Simbas, they eventually accumulated sufficiently to form their own tribe.

"Ample reports of this phenomenon from the Congo over the past sixty years. Yoruba with Hausa, Watusi with Pygmy, Kikuyu with Bantu. And so on. Some of them were allegedly part of the Mau Mau, but that wasn't so much a tribe as a movement. All the database shows is a thematic legend."

"A *what?*" the blond spat out, looking annoyed.

"Thematic legend," Wanda answered, *more* annoyed at

the interruption. "One that retains its characteristics regardless of jurisdiction.

"Essentially, *this* one was that, originally, the Simbas were freedom-fighters who had to flee to the bush when the invaders had them outgunned," Wanda said, with a quick glance at Tracker. "The term 'invaders' probably originally meant 'colonialists,' but its usage has changed over time—probably because of mercenary raids on specific targets." She turned in her chair, looked meaningfully at Cross, and returned to her narrative:

"The Simbas were classic hit-and-run guerrillas. They can be distinguished from the modern version easily enough. Unlike, say, the FARC in Colombia or the Shining Path in Peru, or the Maoists in Tibet, they—"

"We don't need to know what they're *not*," the blond man said, fussily impatient.

Wanda continued as if no one had spoken. "They do not recruit, they permit no looting, rape is punishable by death, and there is no enforced membership. Their minimal requirement—and this is only a rough translation—is that a prospective member must bring a 'hard' part of their enemy as an offering."

She ran her right hand over her hair, as if to smooth it down. "Even the deranged creatures created by that so-called witch doctor Joseph Kony—the Lord's Resistance Army—even *those* kidnapped and drug-crazed children fear the Simbas.

"Their trademark never varies. It . . . well, you've seen the pictures."

"I wonder . . ." the blond mused. "Could that be the link?"

"Africa?" Tiger asked.

"Why not? They had to start somewhere. Maybe they started killing for what they thought was a good enough reason and just got to like it. That *does* happen."

"Yes. I have seen it myself," Tracker said, coldly eyeing the blond.

"Come on," Cross said, in a tone somewhere between tired and bored. "Started in Africa, huh? Wasn't that what you government idiots were saying about AIDS? I mean, before everyone found out it was a lab experiment gone wrong in Haiti?"

"We have confirmed signature kills all over the globe," Wanda answered, looking straight at Cross. "I don't see how it would be possible for unacclimated Africans to strike in the Arctic Circle. Do *you?*"

"Maybe they evolved," Cross said. "Same way we all did, right? Humans, I mean. Some seeds grew in the sun, some in the ice. Or we started in the Cradle, like a lot of scientists think. Places get too crowded, people move on. Especially when they get a lot of encouragement. When's the first confirmed kill?"

"It is difficult to determine with any degree of accuracy," Wanda acknowledged. "We have references to similar multiple slaughters throughout history. Cave paintings of Neanderthals looking up at hanging corpses, looking *puzzled*, as if the killings weren't their work. Egyptian pharaohs left what *could* be records of something similar, unearthed by tomb robbers. Hannibal kept a journal on his way over the Alps. And there are a number of references in futhark—"

"What?"

"Scandinavian runes—probably dating back to early Viking times," she said to the blond man, now *seriously* annoyed at the interruption of her report. "The references go as far back as *we* can go. But, with so many other myths and legends *dis*proven, it's impossible to tell for sure. No way to come up with authenticated facts."

"So those so-called Seminoles could be . . . they could be from the same root?" Tiger wondered aloud.

"Of course," Wanda replied.

Tracker was silent.

"Junkyard dogs," Cross finally said. "They've probably formed into their own species by now." He looked up at the blond man: "I still don't know what you want from me."

"A specimen," the blond man answered, in the same tone he would use to order room service.

♣

CROSS SCANNED the blond as he would a snake he'd never seen before. He couldn't identify the snake, but some deeply rooted instinct warned him that it was poisonous.

"I don't do that kind of work," he said.

"Yes, you do. We don't have time for games. You're a man for hire. And the job doesn't matter if the money's right—we've seen your résumé."

At a nod from the blond man, the large screen started running a "Greatest Hits"-type trailer: Cross moving stealthily behind a young man wearing a ski mask who was aiming a recurve bow armed with a barbed arrow at a giraffe in a zoo enclosure; Cross and another man—short, squat, implacable, casually holding a butcher knife—speaking to a man handcuffed to a desk; Cross in an Amazon jungle, walking point at the head of a small squad. . . .

"*That's* supposed to tell you . . . what, exactly? All that proves my point. I'm a problem-solver, not a hit man," Cross said. "A guy like you wouldn't know the difference, but"—turning to the Indian—"I thought *some* of you would."

"I know the difference." Tracker spoke quietly. "It is also what I do. As Wanda just said, even these 'Simbas' appear to have rules governing what they are permitted to do. But this isn't a contract kill we're talking about. It's . . . it's another war."

"If it is, you're no draftee."

"No. As you said, for me, it is personal. For Tiger, too. Wanda and Percy, they're just lifers."

"Tribalism," Cross said quietly. "The curse of Africa. Spread until it became the curse of humans."

"Never mind the philosophy," the blond man told him. "You in or out?"

"What's 'in' mean, pal? What's the objective here?"

"A specimen, remember. Not a dead body . . . a live one. There has to be a way to . . . deal with them, but we need to study one of them to find out how. No negotiations. You can name your price. But this job is purely COD."

♣

CROSS SAT, thinking it over. Replaying in his head all the assignments he'd undertaken over the years.

Not a hit man—who am I kidding? he thought to himself, keeping his face a show-nothing mask.

"Why me?" he finally asked.

"Believe it or not," the blond man told him, "what we want is your mind, not your combat skills. You have unique . . . experiences that our superiors believe would be invaluable."

"Two choices: either actually say something, or drive me home, pal."

"Look around you, Mr. Cross. Tracker got his name from his work. Percy's been in more wars than I've had birthdays. And Tiger . . . well, she's earned her name. Between our financial resources and the commitment of our volunteers, we have more than enough manpower."

Tiger raised an eyebrow at this last word, but didn't deign to speak.

"Okay, you'll pay the freight, but only COD. Fair enough. But it's not only money I work for. How high do you guys reach?"

The blond man made a gesture which instantly translated to: "All the way to the top."

"Yeah? Can you fix me up with a Get Out of Jail Free card?"

"What's that?"

"Just what it sounds like: immunity from prosecution. The feds do it all the time. They do it for rats; why not for . . . contract employees?"

The blond man exchanged a look with Wanda. "We could probably handle that. Give us the details."

"Details?"

"When the crime was committed, who was involved, that kind of thing."

"It hasn't been committed yet."

"What? That doesn't make any—"

"My crew are all tightrope-walkers. You can't make too many passes without taking a fall. Sooner or later, that happens—maybe to one of us; maybe to us all. So that's what I want: the *next* fall, on the house."

Another look between the blond man and Wanda. Finally, the blond said, "We'll have to check on that."

"I can wait," Cross told him. He slid a slip of paper across the table. "These people'll know how to reach me. Or you can track me down yourselves, in case you want to show off your toys again."

"Tiger and Tracker will take you back," the blond man said as the Indian slid behind Cross, a black blindfold in his hands.

♣

ALMOST DAWN. A limo-sized four-door sedan made its way through the city. It moved purposefully, a shark attracted by the electrical pulses of potential prey.

The comparison is valid. This is the infamous "Shark Car," known and feared throughout the Badlands. A three-ton armored beast, all-wheel drive with adjustable power distribution, independent suspension all around, air bags under each wheel. The power plant was a totally reworked mega-monster engine: a thirteen-plus-liter Hemi, with two separate shots of nitrous oxide always available. Its city-camo paint was a shaded, blotched gray-black, rarely noticed except by those who knew what they were actually viewing.

The high-tech van was on the move as well. Tiger was behind the wheel, Cross next to her in the front seat, the blindfold still over his eyes. Tracker was riding behind them, a short-barreled, night-scoped rifle across his lap.

The van moved placidly through constantly changing neighborhoods. Multi-levels yielded sharp contrasts as antiseptically wealthy sections became festering-sore slums. The lines of demarcation weren't always so clearly marked, especially in newly gentrified areas. Desolate poverty ran through the near-deserted night streets as randomly as the broken veins in a wino's nose.

"What you said before. About tribalism. Was that just playing games with that government stooge?" Tracker asked.

Smoking a cigarette with the black blindfold still in place, Cross looked like a man facing the firing squad. He answered without turning around.

"You tell me. Doesn't this feel like one tribe's doing all the killings? They got their own way of doing things, their own gods to worship. . . ."

"But how could one tribe . . . ?"

"You wouldn't have said what you did about Seminoles unless you've got Cherokee blood yourself," Cross answered.

"I do."

"But you're not *exactly* a Cherokee, right?"

"I just said—"

"You're a Chickasaw," Cross interrupted, speaking as if simply stating a fact. "Which means your ancestors didn't sow crops. Didn't do a lot of hunting, either. So they had to keep on the move."

"Speak clearly," Tracker said, his voice just a shade off threat.

"Okay. How's this? Your ancestors got what they needed from other tribes. And not by trading. They *took* what they needed."

"That was the truth," Tracker finished. "Yes. I see what you speak of now. The Simbas—"

"Tribes wander," Tiger interrupted, speaking aloud what she had been thinking ever since Cross used the word "Simbas."

Cross nodded a silent affirmative.

"Some tribes don't even have a homeland," Tiger rolled on. "Nomads. They just pitch their tents wherever they are. Like the Mongols. Or those Chickasaws."

"Yeah, there's no racial piece in this," Cross agreed. "Look at the Gypsies. Like the ones they tried to drive out of France. Had them standing in line for Hitler's ovens, too."

Tiger's "uh-huh" was more growl than speech.

"And you don't have to be Roma to be a gypsy, do you?" Cross finished.

As Tracker silently nodded agreement, Tiger looked over at Cross, thoughtfully. "Right," she agreed, her voice so soft it was almost a purr.

♣

"**ARE YOU** guys the whole team?" Cross asked.

"What team?" Tiger responded warily.

"Whatever Blondie's in charge of. There's five of you that I met. All I'm asking: are there any more?"

Tracker and Tiger exchanged looks. Tracker shrugged his shoulders in a "Why not?" gesture.

"The op is multi-national," Tiger told Cross. "We're Unit 3. I don't know how many teams are working this, but I can tell you this much for sure: there's no place where the killers we're looking for *haven't* made an appearance."

In her mind's eye, Tiger reviewed footage she'd been shown of other units. Some seemed racially homogenous, others were overtly mixed, but it would take an expert eye to discern between the Japanese, Korean, Thai, Laos, Vietnamese, and Chinese that formed one group. Assembling a *team* from those nationalities had never been accomplished— their traditional posture toward one another has historically ranged from simmering hostility to outright warfare.

It was the same for a black crew. A closer look would reveal members ranging from Africa to the West Indies. A Latino unit had Mexican, Cuban, and Central and South American members—the latter still another example that flew in the face of any attitudes known to the authorities. Or the underworld.

"Who's the boss?" Cross asked.

"TRAP," Tiger said, glancing at his blindfolded face. "It isn't a person, it's a program. A computer program. We all feed to a central database, and instructions come back."

Tiger's mind viewed a super-computer, encircled by a waist-high band on which terminals sat. Behind each terminal an operator was incessantly inputting, examining, then inputting again and again.

"A computer . . ." Cross snorted. "Computers don't understand hunter-killer teams."

"It was TRAP that told us to bring you into this," Tiger answered. "Computers don't have to understand, they just have to process. They're no better than the data they feed on. And, sometimes, human 'understanding' would just get in the way."

As she wheeled the van around a long, sweeping corner, it became apparent that they were back in that part of the city where Cross was at home. Tracker leaned forward and unsnapped the blindfold.

♣

CROSS BLINKED his eyes a couple of times. Once sight-oriented, he said, "Drop me anywhere."

The van pulled to the curb. Cross jumped down and slipped into the shadows, penetrating deeper and deeper until he became one himself.

"He knows the old ways," Tracker said to Tiger.

"He knows some new ones, too," Tiger replied as the van pulled off. She flicked a switch to pop a rectangular gauge into life. The activated screen was blank. "See? We lost thermal on him the minute he put on that long coat."

♣

CROSS EMERGED from an alley. The Shark Car was waiting, idling soundlessly. Its back door popped open. Cross stepped in. The car moved off.

"You got them, Buddha?"

"Knew where to meet you, didn't I, boss?"

"I had the transmitter on me—in the heel of my boot. But they'll probably sweep that van, find the little unit I left behind."

Buddha pushed a button. What looked like a navigation

screen opened on the dashboard. A moving red dot was plainly visible. "Maybe so," he said. "But they haven't done it yet."

"Then Rhino has them locked on, too. I guess that's all we can do for one night."

"You really think they might go for that free-pass deal, boss?"

"It's probably not their call. But that doesn't matter. They'll *say* so, anyway."

♣

"**YOU GOT** the package?"

"In the trunk, boss. Right next to the RPGs."

"Okay. We might as well clean up the bear-claw thing. Chang's expecting a visit—his spot's right above that Chinese restaurant. The building is only two stories. He's got all kinds of protection on the first floor, and the upstairs windows overlook the street, so their lookout will see us the second we show—they all know this car."

"So they see it. So what? You'd come by to pick up your money in person, right? Besides, I'll be ready to launch ten seconds after you hit the street."

"Yeah. We really got no choice. Chang thinks we did the job on Viktor. Maybe there's all kinds of questions about how those Russians got splattered, but nobody doubts they're gone. All of them. That's gonna make him nervous. Chang's the kind of guy who hates loose ends. That's why I have to just walk in. Coming to pick up my money, that *is* what he'd expect. So seeing me might calm him down some. And we don't need him calm for long."

♣

"**I HAVE** your payment, Cross. In that silver case, over to my right. But, before you pick it up, would you indulge an old man by answering a question?"

"Depends on the question, Chang."

"Ah. You are a man who never changes, Cross. Very well. There is no question but that you have earned your fee. But one question remains unanswered: *how* did you do it?"

"That I can't tell you."

"And why would that be so?"

"Trade secret."

"To be sure. But do not friends sometimes share their secrets?"

"They might. But we're not friends. Otherwise, you wouldn't have my payment—payment I already *earned*, remember—sitting between those two gunmen of yours."

"I have insulted you?"

"Yes."

"Then I apologize. Perhaps we are not *yet* friends." The old man snapped his finger. One of the men who had been guarding the silver case picked it up and brought it over to Cross. He placed it on the floor, and then returned to his post. "But friendship between us, that remains a possibility?"

"Yes."

"Excellent. Perhaps you would like to open the case?"

"Why would I disrespect you, Chang? You are a man of your word, as am I. *That* was what we both respected when we reached our bargain. This is something we share. So I leave as I came, with promises kept on both sides."

"I understand," Chang said. He moved his head a fraction of an inch. Cross returned the gesture, bowing more deeply, but never below the range of his eyes.

Then he picked up the silver case and walked out of the room.

♣

STANDING BEFORE the passenger-side door of the Shark Car, Cross spoke very softly. "This case weighs more than the other one."

"If it's a trick, it's the last one he'll ever pull," Buddha's whisper came from under the car. By the time Cross had his door opened, the first RPG launched.

The second floor exploded in a burst of flame. The next two rounds hit the restaurant below. The fourth went back to what was left of the second floor.

Buddha slid into the driver's seat. The Shark Car disappeared, paying no more attention to the sirens that tore the night air than did the men in their death-throes inside the building.

"Where's the RPG tubes?"

"I left them behind, boss. Take too long to pull 'em out, stick them back in the trunk. But they've all got timers. Three minutes from launch, each one's going to turn into metal dust."

"Timers . . ." Cross said, looking down at the silver case he was holding in his lap.

"Toss it?"

"There's supposed to be about three hundred K in here, Buddha."

♣

THE SQUAT little man's touch on the steering wheel was as delicate and skilled as that of a concert pianist. The Shark Car ripped through the city, heading for the Badlands. When it crossed the barrier and slid to a stop, Cross jumped out, yelling "Condor!"

A teenage boy with a blue Mohawk haircut popped up,

bending his body around the roll of razor wire that topped a chain-link fence in the pose that had earned him his name.

"See this?" Cross held up the silver case. "I'm going to lob it over. You take it and put it someplace nobody's going to stumble over. Then get away from it as fast as you can. Don't come back to wherever you stash it until I show up again—it could be a bomb, with a timer on it. Got it?"

"Yes, sir."

Cross held the case in both hands, swung it back and forth to build momentum, and released his hold on his last forward swing. Condor caught it in both hands and took off, running through the darkness as if he had infra-red eyesight.

The Shark Car pulled away.

♣

THE OLD man's white hair flowed down to his shoulders. He was sitting in a lotus position, smoking a pipe that looked to have been carved from bone.

"You were not expected," he said.

"I didn't want to say anything on the phone. And I knew I'd be recognized."

"You have something for me, then?" the old man said, smiling a murderer's grin. His gray teeth turned the gesture into an even more deadly grimace.

"I have Chang."

"You are holding him?"

"No. Nobody will ever hold him. I have his life. He's gone."

"I heard nothing—"

"You will."

"We did not retain such a service."

"Consider it a gift. A gift from a friend."

The old man immediately handed his pipe to Cross, who took a deep drag without hesitation before returning it.

♣

THE NEXT day, Unit 3 assembled in the War Room. It was obvious that they had been discussing something for a long time: the place was littered with coffee cups and food wrappers. They all looked various degrees of disheveled, except for Tracker.

"You really think he's worth it?" The blond man's question was directed at the room, not at anyone in particular.

"I believe he . . . understands them," Tracker said thoughtfully.

"He doesn't care," Wanda said. "He will regard it as any bounty hunter would. Only, this time, the 'dead or alive' is limited to 'alive.' "

"Look," the blond man snapped, "we don't have time to keep arguing with each other. We're still 'Unit 3' to the spooks, but the reality is, we've stepped over the line too many times already. . . ."

"*You* stepped over the line, Blondie," Percy fired back. "And you took me and Wanda right along with you. One more mess like over in Indiana . . ."

As Percy spoke, everyone else in the room had a mental picture of him standing spread-legged on a ghetto rooftop, a surface-to-air missile launcher braced on one thick shoulder. He staggered slightly under the kick of the weapon. They saw the vapor trail of the rocket as it unexpectedly veered off-course, its heat-seeker attracted by a closer target. That turned out to be a small private jet, which disintegrated immediately on impact.

They also saw a newspaper headline:

TERRORIST ATTACK AT GARY AIRPORT!

"Things happen," the blond man said, unruffled. "We know they use some kind of heat-seeker themselves. It only made sense to turn the tables."

"I didn't sign on to waste civilians," Tiger said.

"Civilians? That plane was carrying a load of dope dealers, on their way back from Vegas. And if you don't like us bringing Cross in, you can split. Take the Indian with you, too," the blond man told her. "We're on our own now. And we don't have a hell of a lot of time, right, Wanda?"

Wanda checked her computer, nodded. "No. TRAP *will* figure out that we've been mobile-accessing its closed-level data. In fact," she hypothesized, "it probably could have found us already, had we been Priority One."

"And we're not," the blond said, "so what does that tell you?"

"What it *always* tells us," Percy threw in. "We pull this off, the brass says all is forgiven. We don't—we get erased."

The blond got to his feet and started pacing. He turned to Wanda, apparently the one person with whom he had any sort of affinity. "Could we make it happen, what that man wants? Immunity for a future crime?"

Wanda worked over her keyboard. "Some places, yes. Detroit, Cleveland, too. And New York for sure. As for Chicago . . . you know how it works here."

"That'll have to do," the blond said, to no one in particular. He had adopted this habit many years ago, relieving himself of the unwanted feeling that no one was listening.

♣

"**I MAKE** it three-to-one it blows up," Buddha said to the crew watching him manipulate a robot originally intended for disarming bombs. "Be just like that rodent to pay us off in plastique."

Cross said nothing.

"Credit cards?" a thick-necked Hispanic youth mused aloud.

"Not plastic, fool," a small, slender black youth wearing a pair of glasses with one orange lens snapped. "Plas*tique*. Like dynamite, only you can shape it any way you want, like it was a piece of clay."

"All of you, shut up, okay?" Condor hissed. "You know the rules: we get to watch so long as we watch *quiet*."

All the watchers immediately fell silent. Theirs was a gang with no name. None was needed. No rival crew was going to claim the Badlands—the Cross crew was only a whispered rumor to most outlaws, but none wanted to test it.

The gang's members came in all sizes and shapes, all colors and creeds. All they shared were survival skills so finely honed that they were able to permanently reside in an area nobody in his right mind would even enter.

Years ago, a daredevil graffiti artist had accepted a challenge to plant his tag on a semi-trailer that had been stripped of its axles. Now completely coated with a solid layer of rust, the trailer stood only about a hundred feet past the twin piles of crookedly stacked junkyard cars that marked the border to the Badlands.

The tagger knew if he managed to pull off that stunt he'd immediately be crowned as the King of Graffiti throughout the city—a stake worth playing for.

The tagger picked broad daylight for his move, knowing that the darkness which usually cloaked his work would not be his friend on this mission. Besides, maybe only *some* of the rumors were true—whoever heard of a gang that got up before noon?

It was just before ten in the morning when the tagger

stepped behind the pillars of junked cars and advanced on the semi. He carried only two cans of spray paint: one for lettering, the other for outlining. He had no need of any of his usual equipment—there would be no climbing involved in this exploit. He didn't even carry his prized notebook—he could spray his personal tag with his eyes closed.

The assembled watchers on the other side of the border never agreed on what happened next—a cloud of metallic rusty dirt rose like a curtain between their eyes and the doomed tagger. But there was no argument that the body of the tagger came flying at them in a long, high arc, as if it had been launched from a catapult.

The rule was as simple as the skull-and-crossbones on a bottle of poison: you didn't enter the Badlands unless you planned to stay. You might join the gang—provided you proved in according to whatever requirements were current—or you might just have created your own gravestone.

♣

THE NO-NAME gang watched as Buddha deftly moved the controls of the robot, sending it across obstacle after obstacle.

"You picked a good spot," Cross said to Condor. The young man visibly swelled with pride at the praise. He deftly snatched the rubber-banded roll of bills Cross tossed in his direction, and immediately threw it over his shoulder to a Samoan youth whose bulk belied his speed.

The robot reached the silver case. Its long arms tapped their way to the single latch, and popped it open.

Silence descended.

"Go," Cross said.

Condor raced across to the case, picked it up with both

hands so he wouldn't have to shut it, and ran back to where Cross was waiting.

Cross dropped to one knee and methodically played a flex wand with a tiny fiber-optic light at its tip over the contents.

"It didn't blow up," Condor said, unnecessarily.

"You never celebrate a kill until you make sure the body's not breathing," Cross said, softly.

Condor nodded. It wasn't a lesson he would forget. If the Badlands had ever built an idol to worship, it would have looked like Cross.

"Thirteen bars," Cross finally said.

"Looks like Chang was throwing us a bonus," Buddha said, surprised.

"Or setting us up for one," Cross answered. "Maybe he was just staging a scene. There's always a next time."

"Not for Chang, there won't be," Buddha replied.

♣

THE CREW arrived back at Red 71, entering by different paths. They were all inside the poolroom when three men approached. Bowing deeply, they handed Cross a carved wooden stick wrapped in black silk.

Cross returned their bow, after which the three men turned sharply and walked out of the poolroom.

"What's that?" Princess demanded to know.

"A message," Cross told him. "From the head of the gray-tooth crew."

"What message?"

Cross twirled the stick slowly in his hands. "Buddha?"

"Got me, boss."

Rhino took the stick from Cross and disappeared behind the beaded curtain.

♣

BUDDHA HAD dropped three hundred dollars to Princess at the pool table before Rhino returned.

"Some of the symbols are Cambodian, I think," he said. "Nothing matched exactly, but pretty close."

"And . . ." Cross prompted.

"It says either that our enemies are now his enemies . . . or that we can redeem the stick for a body. Payable anytime, and it can be any body we want."

"Now, *there's* a man with class," Buddha said, answering an unasked question.

♣

THE SHARK Car slid into the darkness of a parking lot and spun so that it came to rest with its nose facing out. The view through its windshield was once a large housing project. Its low-rise section had already been converted into expensive condos, but the high-rise buildings were still listed as "slated for demolition."

This being Chicago, "slated" could mean years. In the interim, one of the high-rise buildings had been converted into a major drug supermarket.

The arrival of the Shark Car was immediately noticed by the gang assembled at the entrance to the high-rise.

"Don't those fools know they got to come over *here*, they want to make a buy?" a black teenager with long dreads sneered. "What they think, we gonna send over some bitch on roller skates?"

"Zip it, boy," a far more experienced gangster ordered. He was immediately obeyed. After all, wasn't he twenty-six years old, with nine of those years spent in various lockdowns, a known killer who had embraced the "don't mind dying" credo well over a decade ago and lived it since? In a world where the road ahead forks just once—the jailhouse or the graveyard—he qualified as a tribal elder.

"You know them?" another youth asked the leader.

"Yeah, I know them. You better know them, too."

"Why would I—?"

The speaker stopped mid-sentence, awestruck. His eyes were riveted to a man climbing out of the back seat of the Shark Car. He was looking at a creature from another world: a man whose body was so outrageously muscled that it looked like a comic-book creation. The creature's head was shaven. Despite the evening chill, he wore only a Day-Glo lilac tank top over a blousy pair of baby-blue parachute pants. A diamond bracelet flashed on one wrist; a watch with a huge luminescent face graced the other.

But none of that shocked the youth as much as the creature's face. He wore conspicuous rouge on his cheeks and a liberal supply of eyeliner, and his mouth was slathered with pink lip gloss. A long earring dangled from his right ear.

"That . . . can't be."

"Oh yeah, it can," the elder said. "You looking at Princess himself, boy. The real thing."

"Princess?"

"That's his *name*, fool."

"He's a—?"

"Don't fall for the costume," the elder warned, now addressing an ever-gathering crowd. "All you got to know about that man over there is that he is a stone *beast*. Stronger than a team of oxen, and crazier than a flock of loons. Totally in-*sane*. He dresses up like that so he can get people to jump him."

"What?"

"Like I said, crazy to the max. The only screws he *don't*

got loose, they entirely *missing*. Understand? To that maniac, the other guy has to *start* it. Otherwise, he don't do nothing.

"Listen close, now. That . . . thing over there, you can even call him out of his name, he still won't make a move. But if you move on *him*, you as good as gone. That man so strong he could kill a refrigerator."

The leader looked around carefully. Then he directly addressed the younger man. "You think I'm blowing smoke, you think a man looks like that can't tear you apart, just walk over and bitch-slap him."

"Bitch-slap him with *this*," another young man boasted, pulling a 9mm semi-auto from his belt. "What he gonna do then?"

"Put that away, fool! You show steel to those guys and they make you a corpse. Guaranteed."

"What guys?"

"That's the Cross crew in that car, youngblood. Or some of them, anyway. Trust me on this—your dinky little nine wouldn't make a dent in that car, not even in the glass. And whoever's *in* that car, they packing heavy enough to level this whole damn building behind us."

"Damn!"

"Damn is right, bro. They been around since forever. You ever hear of the guy they call the Ace of Spades, over on the South Side?"

"The hit man? The one who walks around with a sawed-off around his neck?"

"Himself. He's an OG of that crew. Him and this white dude, Cross. Word is, they hooked up Inside. Same place I did time in myself," he added, with an undertone of pride. "They been together ever since."

"He's in that car?"

"How would I tell? Look through that black glass? I'm trying to school you and all you do is ask me dumb-ass questions. Listen! Just learn this much and you be fine: you don't want *no* part of no*body* you ever see in that car. Case closed."

"So what they doing—?"

"Fine," the elder says, in the resigned voice of a man having to prove the obvious. "Just stay here. I mean, don't *move*, you hear me?"

With that, he walked toward the Shark Car, hands held in plain sight. Held open and extended from his sides.

♣

THE OTHER gang members watched as their leader approached the driver's side of the Shark Car. The window must have been down, because they saw him carefully place both hands on the sill.

No sound reached their ears.

Their leader backed away from the Shark Car, then moved toward his gang, hands back in the classic "I'm no threat to you" position.

"They got business here" was all the leader told his crew.

"They didn't pay no tolls."

"You making me *real* tired, young boy," the leader said. "*Tolls?* They wanted, they could've cut us all down like *this*"—snapping his fingers—"only they wouldn't even make *that* much noise doing it."

"We got—"

"Some chumps have *got* to learn the hard way. Listen! The hard way with those guys is you stop breathing. I can't let you make those kind of mistakes. They didn't pay no tolls to park in our place, right? And that's what we all about, right? Money. Am I telling the truth?"

"That's my *name*," the teenager with the pistol said.

The leader reached in his shirt pocket and extracted a

playing card: the king of clubs. He showed the card to all the young men standing close to him.

"King. That means 'ruler.' And that's us. Never mind that *Amor de Rey* crap from the PRs—they at least got enough sense to stay over by Humboldt Park, where they belong.

"Now, you say you all about the Benjamins, right? Okay, Big Money, I got this deal for you. I'm gonna walk a few feet away . . . just over to there, see? I'm gonna stand by myself and hold out this very same card in my hand. You ain't gonna *hear* nothing, but the guy I spoke to—Buddha, that's their driver, *and* the best man with a pistol in Chi-town—he's gonna put a round right through the middle of this here card.

"He misses, everyone who gets down gets paid. He misses bad enough to hit me, that's my problem."

"Everybody gets paid . . . what?"

"Whatever they put up," the leader told the growing crowd, taking off his jacket and spreading it on the ground. "You said it yourself—nobody plays for free. Not here, not nowhere."

♣

THE LEADER walked about twenty paces to his right, then stopped. Bills poured into the lining of his jacket, as more and more of the watchers jumped to get in on the action.

The clump of young men watched as their leader held up the playing card, face out: first to his left shoulder so all could see, then at the extended end of his right hand.

Three seconds passed in dead silence. None of the watching crowd heard a sound, but suddenly they saw the playing card fluttering into the night air.

The leader who had been holding the card never noticed a clump of pulsating shadow at his feet. Nor did he hear the word "Nah" in a dialect he would have recognized as his own had his ears been able to pick up an outside-human-range harmonic.

He retrieved the card from the concrete ground, looked at it with satisfaction, and carried it over to the waiting crowd.

The king of clubs had been center-punched by some kind of projectile, clearly displaying what all recognized as the characteristic pucker of a bullet wound.

"Never saw one that small," one of the young men said, careful to keep his voice on a note of wonderment, avoiding any hint of challenge.

"That's a NATO round," the leader told him, confidently. "Like a .22, but much faster. They for rifles, but Buddha's got his carry-piece chambered for them."

"Man can shoot like that, he don't need no big slug," one of the teenagers said, trying for a sage tone of voice. "Put a slug in your eye, you *are* gonna die."

The leader slapped the young man's upturned palm, acknowledging the correctness of his observation.

"Cost you all some cash," he said, glancing down at the mountain of greenbacks piled up on the inside lining of his jacket, "but that's *all* it cost. And now you know—you ever see that car, see it *anywhere*, you don't run, you stand still. *Real* still. If it's you they want, you dead no matter what you do. But if it's someone else, reaching for your protection could get you good and dead. You get in their way, you never get to stay. Feel me? Feel me *now?*"

The crowd all murmured some form of assent.

"Pick up *my* money," the leader ordered one of his flock. "I get it from you later."

With that, he walked over to the crumbling ruins of what had once been the entranceway to the building which now housed only drug merchants. Leaning his back against this support, he massaged his right wrist with his left thumb, as if to shake the muscle memory of how close Buddha's silent bullet had come.

When he stopped rubbing, the still-pristine king of clubs hidden in the sleeve of his Chicago Bulls sweatshirt was fully dissolved into an unidentifiable dark smear.

♣

MINUTES LATER, a shouted "Five-O!" rang out from behind the leader's crew as an "unmarked" pulled in next to the Shark Car.

"Chill!" the elder commanded. "This ain't nothing about us. Not with that Shark Car sitting there."

A man got out of the front seat of the unmarked-but-obvious police car. He walked toward the back as the rear door of the Shark Car opened and another man stepped out.

Detective Mike McNamara, the legendary confession-coaxer of Cook County, and the man-for-hire known as Cross spoke to each other, too softly for anyone to hear, shielded from view by Princess's bulk.

The hyper-muscled man in the outrageous makeup began to juggle three baseball-sized objects. He handled them so expertly that it was clear this was an old act for him. Not so for the drug-dealing gang, which watched in utter fascination, now completely distracted.

Cross and McNamara returned to their respective cars.

The unmarked pulled out.

The man called Princess caught one of the balls he was juggling in his right hand, flicked his wrist, and lobbed it in a long arc, high over the heads of the youthful gangsters. He instantly repeated the move twice more, so that all the balls were simultaneously airborne.

They were still floating in the night air as Princess dove into the Shark Car, which barked its tires once and was gone.

Several of the gang were still reaching for their guns when the first grenade hit, tearing chunks out of the upper-story bricks behind them.

♣

"**YOU** *HAD* to do that?" Cross said, his voice suggesting that he had said the same words many times before.

"I was just having fun," Princess said, sulking. "Buddha had fun, and you didn't say anything to him."

"Never mind," a high-pitched, squeaky voice came from the back seat, soothing the hyper-muscled man. That same voice was then directed at Cross, with just a touch of annoyance. "You know how easily he—"

"I know, Rhino," Cross said, addressing a huge dark mass taking up virtually every inch of the back seat that Princess wasn't using.

"Why don't you just buy him a damn Xbox or something?" Buddha growled.

"What's an Xbox?" Princess asked excitedly.

"Thanks a lot, Buddha," the dark mass squeaked sarcastically. "Maybe your wife could give me some shopping tips. Like where to pick up a bargain, you know."

"Hey! That was low, man."

"Enough already," Cross snapped, calling a temporary truce in what he knew to be an endless war.

♣

JUST BEFORE daybreak, the Shark Car backed into what was once a garage.

The gang elder's arm emerged from the shadows, a paper bag in his hand.

"Almost twenty G's," he said, very quietly.

"My share."

"I still don't see why you can't be more righteous about that, brother. I mean, I got to set up the whole scene for us to cash, am I telling the truth?"

"No," Buddha told him. "You passed on *that* chance. I offered you, right? Just hold your hand steady and I'll do it for real. You know I can—you were there when I did it with Horton's cigarette a few years ago."

"A man died behind that."

" 'Behind that' was right. He wanted to stand behind Horton, make sure the game wasn't fixed. Not my fault."

"I ain't saying it was. Just saying *like* it was, man. A man should get paid for the risks he takes. I mean, Horton, he *didn't* get hit, but the boy *still* ain't right."

"I already gave you the chance to split the take. Standing offer. Next time, just hold up the card and I'll put a hole in it. Now, *that* would be fifty-fifty. But you wanted to play it safe. Think of it like buying insurance."

"What I need insurance for if you never miss?"

"Calms your nerves," Buddha said. "Ask Horton. But anytime you want to cancel the policy . . ."

Five seconds of silence gave Buddha the answer he expected. The Shark Car slid away from the empty garage bay as silently as its namesake.

♣

CROSS SAT in a working-class living room, facing a man and his wife. On the mantelpiece was a large color photo of a young boy and his dog.

"I still can't believe they would do that. Our own government," the man said. He was in his early thirties, a man who had worked hard at hard jobs all his life. "I fought for them in the desert. I did everything they asked, every damn time.

And now I'm a cop. I spend every night riding around in parts of Chicago that people shouldn't even have to live in. If *I'm* not an American, who the hell is?"

His wife leaned against him, as if the touch of her body would give him emotional support. She was a short, red-haired woman, a couple of years younger than her husband. Years ago, his high-school sweetheart. Once, she would have been called pretty, but recent events had aged her.

"It won't bring our Bobby back, Bill. It wouldn't change anything. . . ."

"Yeah, it would. You *know* it would, Ginger. He has to pay for what he did. I just can't believe our own government is protecting a creature like him."

"Really?" Cross said, pointing at a small TV monitor he had brought with him. He pressed a button, and tape started to roll. The patched-together montage was a review of the only known facts:

Their son had been kidnapped. The child's body was found ten days later, carelessly dumped behind an abandoned factory which had outsourced all its production. The unmistakable marks of torture on the child's naked body turned the autopsy shots into the worst kind of kiddie porn.

"Profilers" had contributed such a generalized portrait that it would fit at least 10 percent of the city's population. The local police had checked the Sex Offender Registry and found numerous individuals they wanted to talk to . . . but more than half weren't at the addresses they had supplied.

What the monitor did not show was a detective standing before a uniformed patrolman. The detective would have been called handsome by anyone who failed to notice his ice-cold eyes. Even if his hands had not been scarred, even if his nose had not obviously been broken and reset several times, the detective's body-balance would have revealed him as a skilled martial artist to any true practitioner.

Nor did the monitor show that same detective later speaking across a table to a gentle-looking, well-dressed man. Or the detective smiling a cobra's grin, speaking with a faint Irish brogue as he told the man across from him, "Well, you know how the game is played. You *should* know by now. The more you put on this stack"—his hand touched a single piece of paper to his left—"the more we can take off this one." The stack of paper to the detective's right was about half a ream thick.

What the monitor *did* show was headline after headline, as members of an international ring trafficking in children— live and on film—were exposed, imprisoned, and, in one case, shot and killed when attempting to grab the arresting officer's weapon. Internal Affairs had cleared the officer after a thirty-minute investigation.

"You know what that slime got in exchange for informing on a whole bunch of others just like himself?" the man said to Cross. "Ten years. And, for a bonus, he won't even have to serve it in Protective Custody. The feds changed his name and got him plastic surgery. He's doing time, but in what they call a Level One prison. He couldn't be in a safer place—nobody wants to be sent away from that country club to a real prison."

An old Labrador retriever limped into the living room. "Good boy, Duke," the man crooned softly, patting the dog's silky head.

"He still grieves for Bobby," the woman said. "He still waits for him to come home from school. Every day."

"No. He *knows*, Ginger," the man said to her. "Hell, he took a bullet trying to protect him, didn't he?"

The man's mind saw only what he had been told by brother officers. As the kidnapper tried to haul the boy into a car, the Lab sprang at him, tearing at the abductor's flesh before a bullet made him drop the bite. Wounded but undeterred, the Lab crawled after the fleeing car, not stopping until he collapsed from loss of blood.

"If it wasn't for that dog, we wouldn't have had a thing to go on," one CSI team member said to another as the Lab was being loaded into an ambulance.

"Duke had that filthy . . . *Huh!* I was going to say 'animal,' but that's not right. Not fair. How could I even think something like that when *Duke's* an animal? I don't know what to call a . . . thing like him, but Duke not only had a piece of his sleeve, he had his DNA all over his teeth. And it *still* took them over three weeks—"

"Bobby was . . . gone right away, honey," his wife said, patting her husband's hand. "It wouldn't have mattered."

"Matters to *me*," her husband managed to say before the tears came.

A cheek muscle jumped in Cross's otherwise flat face. Something was clicking inside his criminal mind, but he wasn't sure what it was . . . yet.

He patiently waited for the husband to regain his composure.

"That maggot's safe," the husband finally said to Cross. "I'm sorry we wasted your time. I don't even know why McNamara gave me a number for you. But everyone on the force knows Mike Mac's the best cop there is. And that he knows those . . . kind of people. But even he doesn't know what name the feds gave Bobby's killer. Or where they've got him stashed.

"Besides, how could you get to him in a prison like that? Stateville, sure—you can get a man done for a couple of cell phones. But in a luxury palace where they'll kick you all the way down to Supermax if you screw up . . ."

The man got to his feet and offered his hand for Cross to shake. "I don't expect you to pull it off. I get that. Mike

Mac told me the deal: no promises. But if you ever do find out who he is now, just tell me. Get me a mug shot. I'll wait. After all, it's only ten years."

His laugh was bitter enough to make acid taste like honey.

"You won't have to," Cross told him.

"Won't have to . . . what?"

"Wait," Cross said, turning to leave.

♣

"**YOU ARE** certain of this?" The speaker was Corsican, an old man immaculately dressed but without a trace of flash to his perfectly tailored dark suit, worn over a white silk shirt with a black tie. A funeral outfit.

He was seated at a table for two inside Red 71, facing Cross. A lifetime of survival had taught the old man a great deal. He looked into the eyes of the man so physically close to him, but all he could see reflected in the irises of those eyes was the message that, whoever you might be, life—*your* life—meant nothing to him.

Whoever pays him first, the old man thought to himself. Aloud, he said: "There was little time, unfortunately. How such filth could have learned . . . Ah, it is not important, *n'est-ce pas?* But know this: he is hated by many. I will not lie. Some hated him for what he was, but others, they actually did business with him. And now they rot in prison. In most cases, this hatred would be an advantage. But it was *because* this creature is so hated that he is now so protected."

"I know."

"And yet you—? Ah, that, too, it is of no importance. I am an old man. My mind rambles. *Pardonnez-moi.*"

Cross's only response was to light a cigarette.

"How much will you require as an advance?"

"Not how I work. The total gets deposited. You know with who. When the job is done, the money gets released to me. I don't get it done, it gets returned to you. Every dime."

"We have a contract," the old man said. He did not offer to shake hands.

♣

AT THE top of the stairs, the old man gave his two bodyguards a meaningful look. He had expected they might be searched. Instead, some kind of human beast had simply pointed a banana-clipped rifle at them. He held the rifle in one gigantic hand, as another might hold a pistol.

The monster gestured toward a pair of what might have once been sofas. His message was clear: Only the old man could go downstairs. His bodyguards could stand; they could sit; they could reach for whatever weapons they might be carrying—it was all the same to him.

The old man had long ago learned to mask fear with anger or disgust. *"On s'casse! C'est une baraque de dingues!"* he barked, deliberately moving out of that den of horrors before his bodyguards could bracket him properly. Sending the message that, once inside *that* place, you were unprotected, no matter who or what you brought with you.

As the three men walked through the mini junkyard surrounding Red 71, a piece of concertina wire twisted. Only the dogs reacted to the call-and-response mimic of Delta blues, which had morphed into "Chicago style" with the journey north and the switch from acoustic to electric. In that below-human harmonic, it sang:

"Baraque de dingues."

There was a pause. Then:

"Reste."

♣

THE NEXT morning found Cross at the same table, sipping from a glass of vile-looking liquid as he read a newspaper headline:

SERIAL KILLER IN MYSTERY SUICIDE!

The name "Mark Robert Towers" appeared in the type-script beneath, cluttered with vague phrases such as "Perhaps the most prolific serial killer of all time." There was more, all generic versions of the same theme: authorities investigating, isolation-cell safety, speculation about "final remorse."

None even so much as hinted at any possibility that the suicide had been of the involuntary variety.

Perhaps the TV coverage . . .

Cross stood up and walked over to the wooden counter which was always standing sentinel at the bottom of the stairs leading down to the poolroom. The elderly man behind the plank counter did not look up as Cross joined him and changed the channel on the TV set.

The announcer was saying:

"Mark Robert Towers, who had recently confessed to a string of murders throughout the country, was found hanging in his special isolation cell in the Metropolitan Correctional Center. Although rumors persist that Towers was himself a homicide victim, the authorities will only say that the matter is still under investigation. What is clear, however, is that Towers had no contact with other inmates, as numerous threats on his life had been received. . . ."

Cross moved his thin lips in a gesture some might mistake for a smile.

♣

CROSS ENTERED the basement of a tenement. With the aid of a pencil flash held in his teeth, he quickly located the telephone junction box. He lightly touched each pair of connectors with a wandlike device held in one gloved hand. When the wand rewarded his efforts with a greenish glow, he attached a pair of alligator clips, both wired to a handheld phone.

When he heard a dial tone, Cross held a small tape recorder to the mouthpiece and pushed a button. The recorder played a series of tones.

The number he just "dialed" rang.

"*Allô*," a man answered.

"*C'est fini*," the recorder's voice said. Unhurriedly, Cross disconnected the clips, pocketed everything, and left, as ghostlike as he had entered.

As he exited the building through the basement door, the passenger-side window of the Shark Car sitting across the alleyway zipped its side window down and up again: All Clear.

♣

IT WAS the same newsreader, on the same channel Cross had watched in Red 71. The broadcast was coming into the War Room. The blond man yelled over to Wanda, "Get me . . ."

"Already on it," she replied.

♣

AS THE members of Unit 3 evaluated the information that was pouring over their terminals about the serial killer's suicide— "Or was it murder?"—the Shark Car slipped through the city.

"He's here," Wanda said.

"Still wearing his special little coat?" Percy said, his voice heavy with suppressed anger.

"No searches," the blond man warned. "We're fully operational now."

"Fully *rogue* operational," Percy reminded him.

"We can do it," the blond man answered. "And once we bring . . . whatever the hell it is . . . once we bring it in, we'll be properly acknowledged, don't worry about that."

"Maybe by the people you work for," Tiger replied. "Me, I'm not on your payroll—I've got my own scores to settle, remember?"

Tracker was silent. Why repeat that which has already been said?

♣

INSIDE THE War Room, the blond man tried to project an air of assurance. "We can make it happen."

"And you want me to take your word for it?" Cross responded, his face a blackboard immune to the blond man's chalk.

In the silence that followed, Cross reached into the depths of his coat. Before Percy could level the MAC-10 he instinctively pulled, Cross held up a pack of cigarettes.

"No smoking in here," Wanda told him, wishing she had made the statement the last time this cold man had paid them a visit—she knew it was much more difficult to reclaim territory once ceded.

"I didn't light it," Cross pointed out. "I just wanted to share tobacco." With that, he offered the pack to Tracker, who was seated behind him. Tracker carefully extracted a single cigarette before he tossed the pack over Cross's shoulder, confident that it would be caught.

"What the hell was *that* all about?" Percy demanded.

"You would not understand," Tracker told him.

"Try me."

"You don't want that," Tracker said.

"You sure?" Percy fired back.

"Stop it!" Wanda snapped. "When this is all over, you—*all* of you—can do whatever you want, okay?"

"Yes, mistress," Tiger giggled.

♣

CROSS, TRACKER, and Tiger were deep in conversation, with Percy occasionally contributing. The blond man was off somewhere with Wanda. If their absence was a source of concern to those remaining, it didn't show.

"You've got a complete record of their hits?" Cross asked.

"No way we could," Percy said, blunt-voiced. "It's not like they're subtle about who did the ones we know about, but we gotta figure there's bodies that haven't turned up yet. They're probably out making a bunch more while we're sitting here."

"What about that thing . . . with the dogs. There's something there; I just can't pull it out," Tracker said.

Cross felt the current just released. "They ever kill cats?"

"Not house cats," Tiger told him. "Maybe a jungle cat, we couldn't say for sure. But we found plenty of bodies with regular cats around them . . . and the cats were still alive."

"That's the hook," Cross said. "They don't care about—"

"Who?" Percy leaned forward.

"Cats. Cats don't bond to humans the way dogs do. Whoever they are, they only hunt humans. In at least *some* of all those other kills you told me about, dogs were hacked too. The killers came for the humans and the dogs tried to protect them. Nothing personal to the killers—the dogs just got in the way."

"Silent whistle," Tiger said, almost to herself.

"Hearing range, yeah," Cross picked up her thread. "I don't know about cats, but dogs, no question they can hear harmonics humans can't."

"Dogs can hear them coming?" Percy asked, as if the whole picture was finally snapping into focus.

Cross shrugged. "It'd fit, right? The dogs hear . . . whatever this thing is. Or maybe they smell it. Either way, they go right into protection mode. But the humans they're trying to protect wouldn't get that message—they'd think the dogs were snarling at shadows."

"That is why our people always had dogs," Tracker confirmed. "But the . . . Simbas, if that's who they are . . . there's still something almost . . . clean about what they do. It is as if they only hunt hunters."

"Or they only kill killers," Cross narrowed it down.

"What about this one, then?" Percy challenged, pulling out an eight-by-ten photo of a signature-kill corpse hanging from a jungle gym in a kid's playground. "This guy wasn't even armed."

Cross picked up the photo and studied the scene. Flipped it over, read the ID information on the back. "There's info here," he said. "Can any of you except Blondie's girlfriend work that computer?"

Tiger shook her head. Tracker's answer was silence.

"I can't make it sing and dance the way that slope bitch does," Percy said, "but I can get some basic stuff out of it. What do you want?"

"A BCI?"

"Can do," Percy responded, planting his heavyweight body on Wanda's stool. He started banging away immediately, jeopardizing the keyboard with vicious two-finger blasts.

Cross lit a cigarette. So did Tracker.

Tiger said nothing. And missed nothing.

They waited.

"Son of a *bitch*!" Percy said, staring at the screen. "He was a goddamned pedophile."

"A what?" from Tiger.

"Baby-raper," Cross told her. "That's what he was doing in that playground. Hunting. Stalking the ground, picking out a target. You understand?"

She nodded, a warrior's stony mask dropping over her gorgeous features.

"And now *all* of us do," Tracker added grimly.

♣

THE BLOND man and Wanda entered the War Room together. Wanda sniffed at the smell of smoke. But her annoyance instantly vanished at the far worse violation she detected: in her absence, someone had dared to touch her computer. Her dark eyes whipped around the van. Only Tiger reacted . . . with a fake-seductive wink.

"Learn anything?" the blond man asked.

Nobody answered.

"You know what we want," the blond said to Cross. "And *you* want to see a grant of immunity all typed out and signed, with a blank space where the crime should be. With the same exact computer, printer, and paper that was originally used, so you end up with a perfect match. Okay, you've got it."

"Sure I do."

"What kind of proof could we possibly give you?"

Cross put two fingers against his jawline, as if he was

thinking it through. The blond man kept a barely veiled smug look on his fox-face.

Cross snapped his fingers with an "I've got it!" expression on his face. "If you're really all that connected, you should be able to tell me where this guy is," Cross said, pulling an old mug shot out of his coat.

"Who's this?" Blondie asked.

"A baby-killer," Cross told him. "A baby-killer with *real* immunity. New face, new name. He's doing lightweight time . . . somewhere."

The blond man handed the mug shot behind him, without looking. "Wanda . . ."

Wanda snatched the mug shot and placed it on a photo-image enhancer. She pixilated it carefully, then used a digital scanner to break the face into tiny components, each with its own number/letter series. She was playing her keyboard like a first-chair cellist, her face glowing with the joy of the chase.

As she worked, her movements told Cross that this genre of hunting was Wanda's *raison d'être*. As each new piece of information came up on her screen, she reacted in a distinct but subtle parallel to a woman being worked up to orgasm.

NAME/NATAL/GIVEN: SLOCUM, LINDSAY, NMI.
NAME/CODE: INSIDER-KP.
NAME/CURRENT: FELTON, REGINALD D.(ANIEL)

The same process occurred, much more dramatically, with the face itself. Cross watched as it progressed from the original through the various stages of plastic surgery to its current configuration, which bore no resemblance to the original mug shot.

At Wanda's touch, information continued to play across the screen:

LOCATION/U.S. INSTILLED. #11-C
SECURITY LEVEL -1

Wanda hit a final button and a printout flowed into her hands. She handed it over to the blond man, who, in turn, passed it to Cross.

"Satisfied now?"

"You got yourself a deal," Cross replied.

"What does that mean, exactly?"

"It means that I'm gonna do what you want done," Cross promised. "But I got other business first. Now, what else have you got on this freak?"

"The priority—"

"Two things," Cross said, his voice as deceptively transparent as an ice cube. "One, *your* priority doesn't mean a thing to me. Two, as it turns out, I have to do this other business to get something I need to do the work *you* want done."

"Perhaps we could—"

"Shut up and let the man do his job," Percy cut the blond man off.

Tracker and Tiger were silent. That frightened the blond man a lot more than Percy's growling. And he was truly terrified of Percy.

♣

"**NO WAY** I can interview him?"

"Not a chance," the blond told the man at the other end of a phone conversation. "We came to *him*, not the other way around. But we *do* have video of him interacting with us, if that would be any help."

"All right, partner," the consultant said. "Send what you've got over that special little modem of yours—I've got the one you gave me all hooked in. Not just the video, now—

everything you put together before you decided he was the man for the job."

"How fast can you—?"

"I'll call you when I've got something to say," the consultant answered, a split second before he pushed the "end" button on his cell phone.

♣

CROSS STEPPED off a commuter flight, picked up the rental car waiting for him, and drove straight to a pawnshop that was on the permanent Watch List for local law enforcement.

His hair was a tangle of blond curls, and he sported a prominent beauty mark on his cheek. An earring dangled from his right ear on a long chain. Anyone who looked closely enough would see the "ball and chain" symbol for a submissive in a "collared" relationship.

Cross exchanged only a few words with the proprietor. They entered a back room. When Cross left the pawnshop, he was carrying a small suitcase.

A no-tell motel took his cash. Cross changed his clothes, then re-entered the rental car. First, he plugged a memory stick into the car's data-port, disabling its GPS. Then he drove for a little less than two hours, totally fixed on his objective, never noticing the urban grit give way to a scenic countryside.

He arrived at what looked like a college campus. A closer look would reveal it to be a minimum-security prison. Cross, now dressed in a conservative suit, with the fool-the-eye disguise removed, entered the prison, carrying an attaché case. He was processed through, enduring only a scanner—no pat-down searches were required at this security level.

Next stop, the Visiting Room. It was an open plan, no barriers between visitors and convicts. Lots of people were visiting, children playing with their sort-of-incarcerated parents; unarmed guards in neat uniforms circled quietly, observant but lacking the hyper-alertness of security staff in real prisons.

Cross was directed to a corner table. He waited patiently until an inmate walked over to him. The man was tall, slender, handsome to the verge of "pretty," with a pencil mustache highlighted against his café-au-lait skin.

The two men's heads moved very close together; they spoke in barely audible whispers.

"Just get him out to the South Yard anytime after two-thirty tomorrow afternoon," Cross said.

"Man, I don't know if I can do that. It ain't like we tight or nothing—I don't hardly know the dude."

"Save it, Maurice. One, you owe me. Two, talking people into things is your game. And, three, I'll make it worth your while."

"Look here, bro. . . ."

"Wait. There's still a number four."

"Which is . . . ?"

"You remember your old pal Ace? He told me to give you a message: You *don't* get this guy out into that South Yard tomorrow afternoon, you better lock up. For the whole rest of your bit, understand? You can't do that here, so you'll need a transfer. And you'd better tell the Parole Board you'd rather do more time, too. The longer you stay Inside, the safer you'll be."

Maurice nodded, not happy about it, but resigned to the realities of his life . . . one of which was men like Cross.

♣

CROSS WAS in full camo gear, which covered not just his body but his head and hands as well. He worked his way through the hills surrounding the institution he had visited the day before. A quick glance at his watch—13:56—confirmed he still had plenty of time.

Methodically, he set up a sniper's roost. Next, he removed a rifle from its case, found a comfortable prone position, and dropped the heavy barrel's bipod to steady the scope.

A thin smile cracked his masklike face when he saw Maurice on the yard. The pimp was talking earnestly to a white male, gesturing wildly with his hands to emphasize whatever he was saying.

Cross dialed in the man's face, then slowed his breathing. When certain he could get off a round between heartbeats, he slowly squeezed the trigger.

The target's head exploded, followed immediately by the *ccccrack!* of a high-power cartridge.

Cross carefully disassembled his sniper's rig and repacked everything, working quickly but unhurriedly.

Then he made a careful retreat through the wooded hills. He stopped near a big tree marked by a freshly dug trench in the ground, lined with some sort of metallic cloth.

His camo gear came off first. By the numbers. When everything was stowed away, including the sniper rifle, Cross dressed himself in conventional hiker's clothing.

A piece of polished steel confirmed his restored appearance. Cross then removed a pair of large glass-stoppered bottles from behind the tree. As he poured the contents of each bottle into the trench, they formed a new substance, which immediately went to work. Cross watched as everything inside began to liquefy, then carefully resealed the metallic cloth with his gloved hands.

It only took minutes for Cross to replace the divot, check

the scene to make certain he'd left no trace of his presence, and move out.

♣

"**I CAN'T** believe it," the young cop said. "I mean, how could a sniper pick him off at that distance? That's almost half a mile."

"I guess when they say 'low security' that about covers it," McNamara replied.

"That man you sent—"

"I don't know what you're talking about," McNamara answered, using the cold voice he saved for special occasions. Professional occasions. "And neither do you."

"Okay," the young cop replied, his eyes wet. "But I'll never forget it, anyway. And if he ever—"

The young cop stopped himself from saying anything more. The man he had been talking to was already gone.

♣

"**ALL I** can do is give you a stack of rule-outs, partner." The consultant's voice came through the van's multi-speaker system.

"I'll take whatever you have, Doctor," the blond man said.

"For one, he's no sociopath."

"But he makes a living—"

"No offense, my friend. But if you keep sticking your two cents in, this conversation's going to take a long time. I get paid by the hour. And a lot more than two cents."

Tiger giggled. Percy threw his thousand-yard stare. Both aimed at the same target.

"The sociopath diagnosis was ruled out because I couldn't find even a trace of narcissism. And no question but the man has some real loyalty to others. But the absolute tell was when you were able to link him with that car bomb. The target was head of a cartel operating out of Guatemala—the first one to use MS-13 soldiers in America, in fact.

"You don't know who paid him, but no question that Cross brought a whole team down there years ago. The mission had something to do with a diplomat's daughter. Remember, I'm looking at papers with the usual spook blackouts of key data, so that's the best I can do.

"Anyway, Cross lost at least two men in that operation. A narcissistic sociopath might seek revenge because of some 'Nobody messes with *me* and gets away with it' need to maintain his personal reputation, sure. But Cross seems to have been acting based on what the dead men would have *expected* of him. That's the kind of leader professional soldiers would *want* to follow."

"Anything else?"

"From what I can determine, there isn't much to him," the expensive consultant answered. "His personal relationships—male-female, I'm talking about here—seem to be limited to . . . professionals. Strippers. Or, if you like, 'dancers.' That kind of thing."

"He pays for sex? That could—"

"I said 'relationships.' He's not paying for sex. What you'd call a series of 'girlfriends' are all drawn from that same world."

"Doesn't that mean something?"

"Yeah, it actually does. It means Cross only understands people who work for their money, and do that work on his side of the law. Interestingly enough, his original partner—this 'Ace' individual—goes the opposite way. He's had the same relationship with the same woman for a good twenty years. Children, too."

"Does *she* know what he does?" Tiger asked.

"Probably not exactly, but she knows he works nights and never gets a W-2."

"That doesn't really help," the blond man reminded the team.

"Not for what you want, no," the consultant acknowledged. "Oh, Cross can *do* a lot of things, but now he seems to be following some script I can't get at. His whole crew is like a band of guerrillas operating in hostile territory, but I can't see any objective. They seem to hate the government, but they lack any desire to overthrow it."

"Money?" Percy guessed.

"No," Tracker responded instantly.

"He's right," the consultant echoed. "The money's almost secondary to some of the things this crew has done. Taken individually, all might have their individual reasons. But what you have collectively is a gestalt of outcasts."

"A gestalt?" Tiger asked.

"Easiest way to put it is like this," the consultant answered. "The whole is greater than the sum of its parts."

"Could you be a little more—?"

"Remember, I'm theorizing from what *you* supplied," he cautioned. "All right. Of them all, the only one who seems fully centered is Rhino. Why he's taken it on himself to protect Princess, I couldn't even guess at. There's no question that Princess on his own would be as dangerous as a horde of pit bulls on angel dust. *Or* that he doesn't have a malicious bone in that huge body. He's like a child . . . unless some button gets pushed."

"Who can—?"

"Push his button inside the crew? Probably any of them, but only Cross does so deliberately. Once Princess shifts, he's utterly without limits. You really need me to tell you that, after sending me those crime-scene shots? Like the one that shows he *harpooned* a man to a wall?"

"You said you wanted everything," the blond man answered.

"So I did. Okay. Ace is a contract killer. But he and Cross go so far back that how they *maintain* that relationship is a puzzle. Buddha seems to be the most money-oriented of them all. And even Buddha has something else going on. He's that rare individual who likes the chase better than the capture."

"Meaning what?" Percy sneered.

"Meaning, if you put a million dollars on the table as a gift, he'd probably say something like 'Thanks, but I'd rather steal it.'"

"That doesn't provide us with much insight," the blond man said, earning him another round of venomous looks from Tiger and Percy. Even Wanda slid her chair a few inches away.

"Let's try it this way, then," the consultant's voice came through the speakers with a little more of his natural tone, thanks to Wanda's adjustments. "Ace kills for money; that's his profession. Buddha *would* kill for money, but he's got no real interest in killing. Rhino has no hesitancy about homicide, provided it's in furtherance of a specific mission. Princess, however, turns lethal only when he believes someone else 'started it.' That phrase is the one characteristic of his supposedly 'unprovoked' attacks."

"His war cry," Tracker ventured.

"That's about right. As for Cross, there's no question that he'll kill—individuals or groups—without hesitation. But he's not a pure contract man like Ace. In fact, the motivation for a *number* of homicides attributed to him is unknown."

"Could he operate on his own?" the blond man asked.

"Can't tell you. There's no case that it appears he could have pulled off without assistance of *some* kind. But Cross is a man who collects obligations. And he'd call in markers anytime he needed them."

"You understand, for our plan to work, we have to send him in there alone?"

"Sure, I understand. But I'm not sure *you* do."

"What does that mean?"

"It means what I just said. A *lot* of people seem obligated to him, in one way or another. And they all have people obligated to *them*. Cross might walk in there alone, but I'd put my money on him not staying that way long."

♣

LATE THE next evening, the blond man and Wanda entered the War Room. They noted that Cross was already in a whispered conversation with Tracker.

"You tell him yet?" the blond man asked Percy.

"No."

"Tell me what?" Cross said.

"You're going to jail, pal."

Something flashed across Cross's face, less quickly than his left hand disappeared inside his coat. "You got a good sense of humor, Blondie."

"Listen!" the blond man urged. "You saw the news. They hit again. Right inside the Isolation Wing of the federal lockup. The same wing where they were holding that freak who was trying to take credit for the Canyon Killings."

"That suicide?"

"Suicide, my ass. That's just for the media. Towers was one of their signature kills. Here, take a look for yourself."

The blond man tossed several color photographs on the table. Each showed the serial killer who had tried to persuade the authorities he had bodies buried all over the country in an attempt to stave off his own execution. But the man was not hanging as a suicide would be—what remained of his torn-apart body was dangling from some sort of metal hook, both the skull and spine missing.

"Damn!" Cross said, realizing that the complex arrangements he had set in motion with the Corsican had all been for nothing—had he waited another day, he would have been paid anyway. *Just like Viktor's crew*, he thought to himself.

"Yeah, that's right. Whoever did this, *that's* who we want. They've *got* to be locked up right inside that exact same place. That was as up-close-and-personal a kill as I've ever seen."

"Where were they holding him?"

"I told you, in the high-power tank of the federal holding facility. He had his own cell, of course, but all you need to get yourself locked in high-power is be notorious. It actually makes up a large part of the entire institution. Some are in there awaiting trial, others awaiting transfer. So it could be anyone. And there's no reason to think the place was as sealed off as it's claimed, either."

"What makes you think they're still inside? They did their work, why wouldn't they move on?" Tracker asked.

"There's been two more since," Wanda answered. "Inside that same place. Two more killings. Reported as inmate gang violence—stab wounds, lead pipes, like that. But we've seen photos of the bodies. They're in there, all right."

"If you want to hunt hunters, there's no better place . . ." Cross mused aloud.

"Numbers," Tracker added.

"What's that mean?" Percy demanded.

"You kill a killer, all his kills belong to you."

"Huh?"

"Remember what that doctor guy told us? About this being a game? That means someone's keeping score."

"Ah, that was just—"

"How did they manage to get it done? There are cameras everywhere inside that place," Wanda interrupted.

"And that's how we know there's been an insane race war going on in there for weeks," the blond man added. "The body count's already over a dozen."

"You said three—"

"I know, Percy. But only the last two match the signature. And they were both whites. Rumors are flying that there's a special squad of black hunter-killers running wild in there. Keys to the tiers, everything. That joint is a pure terror zone. Way too many guards calling in sick. And they were understaffed to begin with.

"The Aryan shot-caller is a man named Banner. Triple-lifer, knows he's never going to see the outside world. Only reason he's in there is that he's awaiting *another* transfer. Been moved a dozen times. Worthless waste of time—he'll link up in an hour, no matter where they put him.

"The blacks are in a single unit. At least the warriors are. Call themselves the Urban Black Guerrillas. An informant told us that this comes out of their conviction that all prisons are 'cities,' and failure to control their own 'neighborhood' would be a mortal sin.

"There's a loose group of Latinos. And I *do* mean loose. Mexicans and Marielitos aren't ever going to get along, never mind those maniacs from Central America, or local Puerto Ricans. The only good thing is that there's not that many of those. The bad thing is, that's what caused them to band together.

"Even the Asians seem to have called a cease-fire between themselves while all this is going on.

"But we know we're not looking at some convict race war. It's *their* work, for sure. It's like Tracker just said. With all those great targets just waiting—kill a killer, you take all his kills—I think they're going to be around for a while. No point leaving crops to rot in the field."

Cross locked eyes with the speaker. The others watched, expressionless.

"So you see," the blond man finally said.

Cross lit another smoke. "I get it now. Okay, I'll go with it. But there's things you need to do first. And I need a couple of days to take care of some other stuff."

♣

"**WHAT DO** you want for a legend?" Percy asked Cross.

"If I'm gonna hook up fast, I'll need something racial. You got any old Unsolved in there?" Cross asked pointing at the giant computer.

"What do you need an Unsolved for?" the blond man asked. "Those are all cold-cased. Why not just take an open one? A fresh one where they haven't made an arrest? Until you, of course."

Cross gave him a look. "Blondie, you want to go in there, do it any way you like. Only it's *not* you going in, is it?"

Cross deliberately turned to Wanda, making it clear who he believed was the brains of this outfit.

"If you make it a fresh case, especially a race killing, the shot-caller for the gang I have to connect with, he'll probably already *know* who did it. So, if I'm going to claim, then I need an old case, and I need one from out of town—the farther away from that joint the better. Let the feds be holding me for extradition, understand? That way, it'll take anyone trying to check out the crime that much longer. And it'll give you an excuse to pull me out if things get ugly."

Wanda was already at her keyboard. "I've got half a dozen good possibilities," she said. Tiger peered over her shoulder, feigning interest. Wanda's body language clearly indicated she resented Tiger's presence. And Tiger clearly indicated she was well aware of that, deliberately pressing her left breast against Wanda's cheek.

"Okay," the blond man said, confidently. "We'll have this whole thing set up in another twenty-four hours. Anything else you need?"

"Yeah," Cross told him. "A wife."

"Is that a joke?"

"You ever get held waiting trial? Here's how it works: I can get unlimited visits from a lawyer, but they'd get suspicious if any lawyer *I* could afford would come see me every other day or so. Only gangsters can afford that level of representation. The White Power boys might have a local guy, but, remember, I'm on the run, from someplace far away, so I wouldn't know about that.

"Besides, lawyers are way too easy to check out. The only other visits I can get regularly are from a spouse or parent, see? So I need a wife. Someone to come in and visit, carry messages, bring me some stuff I might need, like that. . . ."

"We can't let anyone from outside our group in on this, Cross."

"You won't have to."

"Forget it!" Tiger and Wanda spoke as one.

The blond man turned to Tiger. "If you really want these guys as bad as you say . . ."

"What's wrong with her?" Tiger wanted to know, jerking her thumb at Wanda.

"I can't spare Wanda" was the blond man's immediate answer. "I need her with me . . . on the machines."

"And I'm going in as White Power," Cross added. "I can't have a non-white wife."

Tiger mock-sighed. "They don't have conjugal visits in there, do they?" she asked Cross.

"Close enough." He smiled thinly. "Wait'll you check out the Visiting Room."

♣

CROSS WAS shirtless, reclining in an old barber chair. An ancient Japanese man was working on his arm just below the shoulder, using a needle to which a trio of wires was attached.

"How long is this good for?" Cross asked.

"Ninety days. No more."

"But I can wash it, and it won't come off?"

"It will *never* come off. You will be buried with that tattoo still in place, Cross. It is the ink that I created that makes this possible. In three months, or perhaps a little less, all *color* will disappear. The tattoo will forever be transparent—all that will remain visible will be your own skin underneath."

♣

CROSS SAT in a modern dentist's chair. A black woman in a white coat leaned over his open mouth. She was wearing transparent latex gloves and an opaque face mask. "All finished," she said.

"I can chew on this? Bite down and everything?"

"It's a tooth. It will work like a tooth. When you want it out, you torque your jaw all the way to the side, just as I showed you. Then press your little finger right at the base of the back molar, and it will pop right out, still intact."

"Thanks, Doc."

"Don't thank me. What I just did was for my brother. Flowers on his grave. Our family's debt is paid now, yes?"

"Yes."

"Then don't come back here, Mr. Cross. For anything."

♣

CROSS SAT at a workbench, carefully threading a wire around a thin channel cut into the outside rim of the heel of a rubber-soled shoe. Finished, he began to slowly tamp the thin rubber strip he had razored out back into place. He reattached the heel, holding it up for inspection. Still not satisfied, he added a coat of what looked like black polish, and set the shoes aside to dry.

Hours later, he was in a coffee shop, standing in line. Ahead of him was a young woman who was wearing a dress-for-success outfit, carrying a soft leather briefcase. He handed her a sheaf of envelopes. The return address of the expensively engraved envelopes was that of a law firm. Stamped in red on each one, in block capital letters, was: CONFIDENTIAL LEGAL MAIL.

"You understand what to do?" he asked the woman.

"As soon as I get a cell, tier, and wing number, I send one of these every other day."

"The letters are already written. All you have to do is . . ."

"Make sure they come from our office postage meter," she finished for him, a bored look on her face. "You've already explained it a dozen times."

"You get paid by the hour," Cross reminded her. Then he courteously stepped out of the line, allowing the impatient teenager behind him to be the next one served.

♣

LATE THAT night found Cross talking to an older man with a vaguely Inca cast to his features. They were in a warehouse past the edge of the industrial district, and they were not alone. The place was full of armed men, all with clearly Central American faces.

A regular moviegoer would immediately conclude that this was some sort of guerrilla group. Cross held up a butane lighter, a cheap plastic job.

"They let you carry these things inside?" he asked.

"*Sí!* When you are a pre-trial detainee, you have certain rights. A prisoner in America has more rights than an honest *campesino* in my country."

"Yeah, fine, Ramón. You sure this'll work?"

"Ask *la policía, hombre.*"

♣

THE NEXT afternoon, Cross was seated in the back of a triple-black Jeep, its multi-coat paint gleaming as if polished with oil. A posse car *extreme*, it shrieked "Dope dealer!" from its blinged-out twenty-four-inch rims to its 18-karat neon trim.

The man next to Cross was older, more substantial-looking than the two young wolves who occupied the front seats. He was talking on a cellular phone, but limiting his responses to monosyllables. He put the phone down, turned to Cross:

"It's just like you said—he's working right out of the Community Center. And his partner's a social worker. Damn it! They worked it perfect. We rolled right up on them, sat there, and *watched*. They never even noticed us, but *we* didn't see anything, either. So they got to run their foul game on our children."

The speaker leaned forward to speak to the driver: "Rozzy, swing back up through the edge of where Robert Taylor used to be. Target's located, under surveillance. He's street-side now. If he moves inside, I'll get word. And motor *smooth*, little brother. We don't want him to catch our scent."

As the Jeep cruised through the community, back-mounted woofers and tweeters blasting, the man leaned his face close to Cross and whispered, "We could do this part ourselves, you know."

Cross came back with "It's been a long time between wars, Butch."

"*Between*? Ain't no 'between' for *us*, brother. Don't matter if the canopy's green or concrete, it's still a jungle. Leave one war, you just come home to another."

Cross extended a fist. The other man touched it, lightly.

"We *trying*, man," he said. "But it's a slow go, trying to take back what you never had in the first place."

"That's why you can't take a chance on hosing down the area, Butch. The guys you got now, they're organizers, not shooters. All they know is spray-and-pray. Too much chance of wasting a civilian by accident. And way too many people around here know you by face. Where's *that* leave your program? You know the rule: you always play it the way you planned it."

Butch nodded a reluctant agreement.

"Stealth," he barked. Immediately, the Jeep went silent. No music. Windows closed. Neon trim blinked off. Air-powered sacks over each wheel well puffed out a cloud of black dust, temporarily coating the rims to visually reduce their size.

A few minutes later, the Jeep slid to a stop. Cross got out, wearing an Old-School 8 Ball leather jacket. Bright yellow-orange with a black collar, with a red "8" on the back, it had an elaborate design constructed of separate pieces of leather. The varsity-jacket sleeves had a matching 8 Ball leather patch on each side. Decades ago, these jackets sold for over a thousand dollars, and wearing one out in public was reserved for those who never walked unarmed.

In an era when teens were routinely jacked for their Air Jordans, some of those 8 Ball jackets ended up being worn by those who proudly sported the bullet-hole price-of-possession. Failure to "Give it up!" had cost a number of young men their lives.

Today, such jackets are "collectibles." Which means they never leave their cedar closets.

As the Jeep pulled away, Cross walked purposefully up the street, in the opposite direction.

Ahead of him was a tall black man with spiky hair. He had his hand on the shoulder of a darker-skinned black child: a little girl, perhaps eight years old. Her even younger brother stood next to her, holding her hand. Their tiny figures were dwarfed by the tall man leading them.

Most of Cross's face was obscured by the bill of a low-riding yellow leather baseball cap. And what *was* visible was wildly distorted—the jaw was exaggerated and widened, the tip of the nose extended almost three inches, and hooked to such an extreme that it covered his mouth.

Cross closed to within a half-block from the target, who was still leading the children he had been grooming for months.

The Jeep circled the block and returned to its original drop-off position.

Inside the Jeep, the man in the back reached into a compartment and pulled out a rectangular object. He tapped the driver on the shoulder and said "Go!" very softly, as he slid into position near the window.

The rectangular object turned out to be a video cam. The man holding it muttered, "You like to make movies, dog meat? Good. You about to star in your very own snuff film."

By the time the target sensed his presence, Cross was only a few feet away. The target looked up just in time to see Cross slide a silenced semi-auto from inside his jacket.

The tall man froze. He never saw the Jeep lurking across the street.

The children ran away, still holding hands. They could not have known the danger the tall man was to them, but they were raised on how to react whenever they caught sight of a gun.

Without changing expression, Cross pumped four rounds into the tall man's chest.

A few random bystanders dove for cover, quite purpose-fully *not* looking. Whatever was happening, it had nothing to do with them. If the cops asked them, the shooter was wearing a green overcoat. Or maybe it was a red flannel shirt. And he was either Puerto Rican or Chinese, they couldn't be exactly sure.

Cross reached down, pulled the tall man's head up by his collar, held the pistol to his temple, and blew away the opposite side of his face.

Butch had been filming throughout. He made sure to close in on that last bit, as if a director was whispering "Zoom!" into a cameraman's earpiece.

Cross opened one gloved hand and dropped the silenced pistol on the body. The camera shut off as Cross sprinted for the Jeep.

The street was as quiet as the grave it had become.

♣

LESS THAN an hour later, Cross was inside an office, seated across from the man who had been in the back seat of the Jeep. "You'll get word to them, Butch? Let them know I can be trusted?"

The man gave Cross a level look, pointing at a video monitor in one corner. The snuff film was running on a continuous loop.

"On my life," he said, tapping his chest twice with a closed fist.

♣

CROSS AND Tiger were seated across from each other in a suite at the Four Seasons on Delaware Street, the remnants of their dinner on a white linen tablecloth in one corner. The curtains had been opened to a panoramic view of Lake Michigan.

Tiger was wearing a stylish black dress, low-cut, but not dramatically so. A string of black pearls followed the neckline. Her nail polish was high-gloss black, matching her eyeliner.

Cross was smoking a cigarette, pacing, his tie loosened.

"You got it?" he asked Tiger.

"Yep."

"Everything?"

"Everything."

Cross took a deep drag of his cigarette, eyeing Tiger over his shoulder. "I'm going in tomorrow," he told her.

"So?" Tiger replied.

"So how do you feel about last requests?"

"Well . . . I *do* have a position on the topic. But it's hard to explain. Better let me just show you."

♣

VIEWED FROM the back door of a large courtroom, the judge's bench was centered, set significantly higher than the proceedings below. To his right, sitting behind a "security cage," were several rows of recently arrested individuals, all awaiting arraignment, male and female prisoners separated from one another by a thick steel plate.

Armed guards strutted everywhere, a prominent presence. Their union held the presiding judge in high regard—his ceaseless media demands for better judicial protection had played a major role in their per-courtroom allotment, allowing many the joys of an overtime-bloated retirement.

Two long tables stood in front of the judge's bench stacked with case files running parallel. The left one accommodated a cadre of Assistant U.S. Attorneys—or "AUSAs," as they preferred to be called. They were generally more conservatively dressed than their counterparts on the right-side bench. The Federal Defender lawyers considered the more liberal sartorial standards of their office to be a job benefit. One of the few.

Behind the attorneys' tables were row upon row of spectator seats, mostly occupied by friends and relatives of those about to be arraigned. However, the front-most benches were guarded on each side by stanchion-mounted signs: FOR ATTORNEYS ONLY. There, privately retained counsel patiently awaited the appearance of their individual clients.

The interior decorator's assignment for the courtroom seemed to have been "grim and depressing." The huge room was designed for the mass processing of humans through a recycling system unknown to environmental activists. One far more toxic than anything in a landfill.

An ostentatiously dressed pimp stood in a far corner of the room, rapping urgently to a bored-looking lawyer. "Don't even *go* there, Weissberg—that routine went out with Jack Johnson. I wasn't even in the *car* they drove, and it's not registered to me, anyway. I'd let them stupid bitches stay inside a couple a days, teach 'em how good they got it out here, but how am I gonna pay the fine if they don't keep bringing me my money?"

Clearly, the question was rhetorical. Cash flashed in the pimp's hand, and quickly disappeared into the lawyer's briefcase.

An old-before-her-time Latino woman was talking to a long-haired Federal Defense lawyer, her young daughter at her side. "Javier is a good boy, mister. Those other boys, they . . ." The lawyer nodded, mumbled something about "the system," and turned away.

A well-dressed, portly gray-haired lawyer was massaging a male-and-female couple into a near-hypnotic state, patting the woman's arm reassuringly. "I am quite confident that the court will release Harvey on reasonable bail. However, you must understand, if you don't get him into some sort of a program . . ."

One of the lawyers in the front row was reading a newspaper. A bold-type headline screamed:

EX-CONVICT ARRESTED IN D.C. RACE KILLING!

"We never stopped looking," Detective Jonas Pinkette of the Federal Bias Homicide Squad was quoted as saying. "We knew he was still out there, somewhere."

As a bailiff led three accused illegal aliens away from the bench, the court officer called the next case: "Timothy Arden!"

Cross was led from the pen toward the area between the two parallel benches. A young black man with a sharply etched haircut detached himself from the pool and walked up to meet him, as the court officer recited his hundreds-of-times-a-night, rote-memorized announcement: "No appearance of counsel having been filed on behalf of the defendant, counsel from the Criminal Justice Administration Panel is hereby assigned."

The judge looked down from the bench. Way down.

"Mr. Arden, do you understand what the court officer said? Are you expecting your own attorney?"

"No."

"Mr. Rogers will be representing you for these proceedings, then."

"Him?" Cross said, jerking his head sideways at the black man.

"That's correct," the judge replied.

"No nigger's gonna represent *me*," Cross snarled.

The judge's face flushed, but Rogers didn't seem overly surprised—it wasn't the first time he'd heard such statements.

"Are you saying you waive counsel for arraignment, sir?" the judge snapped at Cross.

"I'm saying I'm not having no nigger for a lawyer. Why can't I at least have a Jew?"

"Very well," the judge interrupted, smugly. "Defendant waives counsel, and will proceed *pro se*. You may step down, Mr. Rogers."

Turning to face Cross, the judge said, "Now, Mr. Arden, you are charged with a number of crimes, including Murder in the First Degree, on a warrant issued out of Washington, D.C., dated . . . 1983. I see this warrant has been outstanding for some time. As I'm sure you've guessed, the District of Columbia has requested your extradition. If you consent, you will be transported back there to stand trial."

"And if I don't?"

"You will be held here, pending a hearing on your return."

"Good. What about bail?"

"What about it, Mr. Arden?" the judge sneered, doing his best *Law and Order* impersonation as he held up his hand to tell the AUSA that no words from him were necessary. "Defendant is remanded. Take him away."

♣

THE BUS chronic recidivists call "Number 13½"—twelve jurors, one judge, half a chance—was intentionally distinctive: dark blue, with broad white stripes running from end to end and across the roof as well. Printed within those stripes, to remind the public what cargo the bus carried: FEDERAL BUREAU OF PRISONS.

Most of the passengers needed no reminder of their status. Earlier that morning, they had shuffled their way to the bus under the wary eyes of shotgun-toting guards. Once inside, they could look out through windows barred with thick steel mesh. A cage stood between them and the driver. Each man was individually handcuffed and leg-chained to his seat.

As the bus pulled away, Tracker lay prone on a nearby rooftop, adjusting his body to adapt to the urban environment as naturally as he would in the mountains. Having attained maximum invisibility, he put a small monocular to his eye. As Cross passed through that lens, he whispered "Loaded" into the mouthpiece of the soot-colored headset he wore.

A shadow shape-shifted at the word, repeating it in Chickasaw, the language of that small tribe of Cherokees who neither farmed nor hunted. Translated it would be . . .

"Stay."

As the bus slogged its way through the city, a pair of playing cards drifted down in its wake: the ace of diamonds and the jack of spades.

♣

THE BUS'S destination was an institution far outside of town, a city-within-walls, housing both "jail" (awaiting trial) and "prison" (awaiting transfer) populations. The bus also carried a few sentenced to that never-specified "felony term" reserved for the constant stream of soft-core Medic-aid defrauders who were filling federal prisons around the country.

Accompanying the bus was a helicopter, a view from which emphasized the sheer size of the receiving institution. A key feature was that there were *no* freestanding buildings inside the walls—they were all connected in one way or another.

However, this particular helicopter was not prison-issue, bearing markings indicating it was a Coast Guard airship. Percy was at the controls. The blond man was in the passenger seat, binoculars to his eyes, scanning. He gestured with his left hand. In response, Percy gently banked the chopper.

On the front console was a grid map of the institution, with certain buildings outlined in bright red. A closer look revealed that some of the tunnels which connected the buildings were actually underground.

"He should be *here* in a few minutes," the blond man said, pointing to one of the red-marked buildings. As he spoke, the bus pulled into a sally port, waited for the gate behind it to close and the one in front to open, then chugged its inexorable way into a small reception area. Men were off-loaded like the cattle the penal system considered them to be. Not 4-H prizewinners, but slaughterhouse beef.

Percy maintained his watch, as talkative as ever. The blond man consulted a number of coded printouts.

♣

CROSS WENT through the Intake procedure with the bored-to-dullness face of a man walking a too-familiar road. What would *not* be familiar to a man whose life had always walked the same circle?

The euphemistically named "Shower Room" offered nothing but a delousing spray. Cross waited as those possessions he was allowed to retain were scanned, standing under a gallows-humor sign which read:

PRE-TRIAL DETAINEES TAKE NOTE:
THIS INSTITUTION IS NOT RESPONSIBLE
FOR THE LOSS OR THEFT OF ANY
ARTICLES NOT CHECKED.

Next was a routine "interview" with a serious-looking young man equipped with a clipboard, who asked his questions as a male inmate nurse drew blood from each man seated across from him. Cross simply shook his head no at each question.

"You have to speak up," the serious young man said. "Otherwise, I would have to *look* up to watch each answer. That would make this take a lot longer. Do you understand?"

"It's not complicated," Cross said, softly, but in a meant-to-be-insulting tone. "If I ever have to answer 'yes,' I'll say it. Otherwise, just assume it's 'no.' So you won't have to strain yourself to look up. Do *you* understand?"

The young man's flushed face revealed his reaction quite clearly.

Cross was walked to a bank of individual cells, flanked by a pair of guards.

"You stay in Iso for forty-eight hours," one told him. "If you test out medically, you go into Gen Pop. You can get some of your stuff back then, too."

"Swell," Cross said.

"You gonna be a problem?" the other guard asked, tightening his hold on Cross's cuffed wrists.

"You treat a white man like this, who knows?"

The guards exchanged a look, but said nothing.

♣

CROSS WAS lying on his bunk, hands behind his head, eyes apparently closed. From behind his slitted eyelids he saw the approach of a white man in a cut-off T-shirt, his bare arms covered in dark ink. The man watched Cross closely, seemed about to say something, then thought better of it. He reached inside his shirt, tossed something on the floor of the cell, and moved along.

Cross didn't stir for a long time, watching as a traffic pattern was established: a porter, moving his mop at jailhouse speed; runners with carts full of reading material; mace-equipped guards, always in pairs.

Finally, Cross picked up the package from the floor of his cell. It was wrapped in a sheet of newspaper—one with the RACE KILLING headline. Inside, he found a pack of cigarettes and a book of matches. And, on a small piece of paper, the hand-printed words: "Your Brothers Are Here."

Cross opened the pack, shook out every single cigarette, lined them all up on his bunk. He carefully disassembled the cigarette pack, then split the individual paper matches. Precautions completed, he lit a smoke and kicked back on his bunk again, watching the smoke drift to the ceiling.

♣

NIGHT IN the Isolation Wing was no different from day. The range of occupants was staggering, but the hardcore thugs were sleeping as peacefully as they would at home. *Back* at home.

Whining, frightened first-timers tried to deal with their anxiety by pacing nervously, nail-chewing, smoking. Some shrieked for help, others just shrieked.

An NFL-sized black man sat quietly with his arms folded, deep in thought. Not pretty thoughts.

A self-described "peckerwood" with a fifties haircut gripped the bars with his hands in the classic pose.

A Latino was busily scratching a heart into the cell wall with a tiny scrap of metal.

Some were crying, as silently as they were able. One paced, clearly contemplating suicide. Another was obviously blissed out on some kind of chemical.

And some were doing a land-office business selling wolf tickets: "You messed with the wrong man *this* time, punk. When they rack the bars tomorrow, you're dead!"

One man screamed, "I'm not him!" Over and over.

"Disciples!" a scrawny black youth shouted, more to bolster his courage than to claim his gang, none of whom were anywhere close.

Outside the cells, a guard watched a bank of small-screen TVs, an earplug in his ear. Most of the screens showed various shots of the Isolation Wing, but only the one displaying some TV "reality" show had his full attention.

♣

TWO DAYS later, Cross was walked through a long corridor, now dressed in an orange prison jumpsuit. For reasons he didn't bother to inquire into, his street clothing had not been returned as promised.

Cross wasn't the only convict in the line. An airlock door slammed behind each of them as one opened in front. This procedure was repeated until all the inmates had been moved to another section of the institution.

"Welcome to Population, gentlemen," a black guard clearly proud of his popping biceps called out, reading from a memo book. "Listen up for your cell assignments. Jones: 7-Down, Cell 12; Rodriguez: 6-Center, Cell 9; Arden: 4-Up, Cell 19: Maxwell; 3-Center . . ."

The discharge area where the guard stood was shaped like the hub of a wheel. The eight spokes, each clearly marked with large numbers over its opening, were the various tiers to which the guard referred. Each spoke had 3 tiers: Up, Center, and Down.

Guards ringed the perimeter. A hexagonal booth was set into the center of the hub, constructed entirely of bullet-proof glass. Inside sat four guards, facing out, each wearing a communications headset.

A mass of inmates had gathered to watch the new arrivals. The "mass" was actually several clumps, divided along racial lines, with an electrically charged space of hatred separating them. As the new arrivals were released to their various cell assignments, they almost magnetically gravitated toward their own racial groups, which absorbed them all until their faces were no longer visible from the center guard-booth. Then all the new arrivals were silently escorted back into the tiers.

Walking next to Cross was a young white male, slender, with a short, once-styled blond haircut. As they entered the tier, a voice floated out:

"Hey, pretty boy! Guess what, baby? You just got yourself a new daddy . . . starting tonight!"

The kid next to Cross flinched involuntarily. Cross suddenly stopped in his tracks and slowly walked over to the convict who had yelled out the kid's future.

"You trying to say something to me?" Cross asked.

"Why you asking?" the convict challenged, surprised at a response from anyone other than the young man he had been working on.

"Why? Because, if you are, you're in the wrong place."

"What?"

"The Suicide Watch is over on the other side," Cross said, deliberately locking eyes with the other man.

That man started toward Cross, fists clenched. But he was intercepted by another white male—older, shorter, but with an air of authority. "Ice it, Tank," the older man said. "He's one of us."

Stepping between them, the older man whispered to Cross through the bars: "You're the guy who blew up that nigger in D.C., right?"

"That's the charge," was all Cross said.

"*RAHOWA!*" the older man replied. "I'm Banner. Commander of the Brotherhood in this joint. This here's Tank."

Cross held out his hand. "About time," he said.

The slender white kid slipped along the corridor to his cell; none of the gangs were watching anyone but Cross and Banner.

♣

"**THIS YOUR** house," Banner said to Cross, gesturing with his hand as if ushering an honored guest into a reception room. The tier had been closed, so the individual cell doors were standing open.

In fact, it was a cell. But, unlike the others, this one was not barren: a full set of toiletries sat on a handmade shelf below the mirror inset above the sink. The toilet itself had a seat made of some sort of thick woven material. The wall featured a couple of centerfold-style pinups. There was a knitted cover on the bed, with a fresh carton of cigarettes sitting on the pillow. The cell gave every sign of having been meticulously cleaned.

"Nice," Cross said, whistling.

"We take care of our own," Banner said proudly. "We got a kite you was coming. And we got a lot of juice with the COs, so it was easy to hook you up in front."

"*Very* nice," Cross said, taking off his shirt. His undershirt was sleeveless. Banner moved in close, making no secret of the fact that he was carefully examining the exposed tattoo.

What Banner saw was a wooden cross. From one of the horizontal bars, a black man hung limply from a length of rope, a noose around his neck. The effect was both terrifying and chilling: a man lynched from a Christian cross. At the base of the cross, there was a series of lightning bolts . . . seven in all.

"Damn!" Banner said. "I never saw one like that before."

"Never?" Cross asked, his tone just this side of threatening.

"Well, I *heard* something about them . . . but I been down a long time. Stuff comes in from the World, you can't always trust it."

Cross moved even closer to Banner, his face almost touching the other man's. An intimately aggressive gesture, deliberately invading personal space.

"White Night," Cross said, very softly. "You ever hear of *that?* Be a good idea for you to ask around. *Then* come back and see me"—making it clear he was dismissing the other man.

♣

THE RIGID requirement that all prisoners had to be locked down each night by ten o'clock was apparently no deterrent to certain individuals.

Late that night, Banner was standing next to a man whose body was covered in whipcord muscle, a pair of thick-framed glasses on his face.

"White Night," Banner ordered the other man. "No, I don't know how to *spell* it. Just find out . . . and find out quick!"

The man with the glasses walked back toward his cell, past a guard who seemed not to notice. Only the sharpest eyes could have detected a folded scrap of paper passing from captive to captor. And everyone was quite deliberately *not* watching.

♣

THE GUARD clocked out a few hours later. He drove to a nearby bar, and ambled over to the pay phone between the toilets in the back.

His call was answered by a man in a quilted smoking jacket, royal-purple silk with black lapels. He was leaning back comfortably in an oxblood leather armchair, surrounded by walls of bookcases. An elaborately framed law degree hung on one bare knotty-pine wall. A bare brunette posed against another.

The man hung up, then punched a button on a phone console. A light blinked in another location. A short, squat man in a room dominated by electronic gear picked up the receiver.

"Yeah," he said, in response to a snapped-out question. "We got someone deep inside, but he's expensive. Real expensive. How high am I authorized to go?"

"As far as you have to," the lawyer instructed.

"And you want it . . . ?"

"Now. Tonight. Understand? *Tonight*, or it's worthless. I have to visit him tomorrow. And I need to have this information when I do."

The lawyer punched another button on his phone console, as if to re-emphasize who was in charge. The brunette recognized the gesture, and slowly slid her back down the wall. A trained dancer, she never broke eye contact with the lawyer as she slowly worked herself into an all-fours position on the plush purple rug.

♣

THE SHORT, squat man was on the phone, speaking urgently. "I don't care *what* it costs. Yeah, it *has* to be tonight. Send it over the modem, encryption 44-A. I'm wiring the payment into your account soon as I hang up. It'll be there in ten seconds. Now, go get what I asked for!"

"Oh, I'll get it, all right," Percy said, after hanging up the phone on the other end. "Sucker."

♣

THE NEXT day, a man who had exchanged an elaborate smoking jacket for a conservative but costly three-piece suit was seated across from Banner in a private conference room. The lawyer was talking; Banner was listening.

"White Night. Night, like the opposite of Day. It stands for the time when every single kike on the planet goes down, and they take the muds and fags with them. Kristallnacht to the tenth power.

"Nobody knows how many of them there are, but word is they're the special enforcement arm for some of the leaderless cells. If this guy has seven bolts under the cross, it means he's done seven hits. Not total—seven for White Night, specifically.

"We picked that tactic up from the Russians. Tattoo IDs, I mean. Not just the usual ink, something you have to *earn*. This guy—Arden, right?—he's an executioner. I don't know what kind of backup he has in here, but one thing's absolutely certain—he's got *total* backing from the top. He's going to *expect* cooperation. Absolute cooperation."

"Hey, thanks, man. You really came through."

"Fourteen Words," the lawyer intoned, leaning forward to shake hands.

Banner watched the lawyer walk out of the conference room, the expression on his face clearly disclaiming any sense of "brotherhood" with a man who memorized slogans but still charged full price.

♣

THE PRISON yard was clearly and sharply divided into sectors. There were, literally, lines painted on the concrete. The tower guards kept their weapons close to hand all the time. And in plain view.

The Latino contingent was off to one side—cohesive, but seriously outnumbered. This wouldn't be the case in Cook County Jail, but in the federal tank, where most of their tribe wasn't gang-connected, just awaiting deportation, they were such a distinct minority that intra-ethnic fighting wasn't even an option.

Despite the summer heat, all sorts of recreational activities were intensely pursued: weight-lifting, handball, dominoes, men walking endless circuits around an oval track, some in pairs. Banner stood in a corner with Cross, a wall of white soldiers between them and the yard.

"Truth is, the way things are now, us and the niggers, we both work the same rackets." Brief glances showed the truth of his statement: unaffiliated inmates were being shaken down, cigarettes were changing hands for pills, a shank was hand-passed from one man to another, all the way down a chain, and all strictly by color.

"We got this joint divided about in half, but even that won't hold—they've been eating away at us over the past few years. All over the country. At least in the federal pens, that much I've seen for myself.

"Used to be we had the whole dope thing wired. Guards wouldn't mule it in for niggers, and their bitches can only carry so much at a time. But those days are gone. There's a lot of major dealers doing time now—they got their own street sources. And don't forget, there's nigger guards now, too. So they pretty much can get whatever *we* can get."

"From what I hear, they've been getting some bodies."

"True enough. They took out that Towers guy right in his cell. No big mystery to that. Guards in here are just like cops on the bricks: there's a price for everything. They most likely didn't do any more than just leave that skinner's cell unlocked."

"Why that one? You taking *his* kind in now?"

"Hell, no! Way we figure it, the niggers just wanted to profile. Send us a message that no white man's safe—they can get to us anywhere. That's why we hit two of them the next day—that was our answer.

"In here, it's just like out there, only it's coming on faster. Race war, that's what I'm talking about. And only one race is gonna be standing at the end."

Banner's words echoed as Cross watched plain-view violence being studiously ignored by custodial staff: everything from fistfights to Pearl Harbor knifings. Nothing had changed from the last time he was incarcerated—firebombing a cell, poisoning food, and battery-packing a sleeping victim are permanent fixtures of prison life. Doing lengthy time was always a multi-color fabric, and homicide its only binding thread.

All conversation stopped as a flying wedge of guards stomped past, double-timing, shaking the ground with the pounding of their heavy boots. They were dressed in one-piece uniforms, body armor, and helmets with full-face visors, mirror-glassed to make individual identification impossible. Each officer carried a see-through shield, shaped so he could maneuver behind it, and a full belt of weapons, including illegal-voltage Tasers.

But no firearms. Not inside the blocks. The Federal Bureau of Prisons' way of saying "Never again."

"Goon squad," Banner side-spoke to Cross, while looking in the direction the squad was running. "Must be some weird stuff going on over there again."

"What's 'over there' mean?"

"That whole block," Banner answered, nodding his head in that direction. "Upstairs, it's PC. Middle is for the psychos. Down is the Death House. Two rows of twenty cells each . . . with the Green Room in the middle."

"Green Room?"

"Used to be the gas chamber, long time ago. Now it's just an empty room. No executions here. For that, they have to move you to a Level Seven."

At the words "Death House," a concrete-colored blotch semi-materialized high up on the wall behind the two men. As the goon squad moved in, "Death House" was repeated at below-human-threshold. Then . . .

"Hit!"

The guards began to club a prisoner repeatedly on his unprotected head, continuing even after the man slumped to the ground, blood running out of both ears.

A mural flashed on the overlooking wall. The ace and jack of clubs appeared, then immediately vanished, leaving some convicts blinking. And the TV monitors blank.

♣

SEATING IN the prison mess room was as radically divided as on the yard, but all races had to pass through the same serving line.

Tension crackled the air. No more perfect opportunity to plant a shank in an enemy's back existed. The convict gangs deliberately ate in shifts—some designated to watch the backs of their comrades while they ate, after which they would change places.

Guards patrolled up and down the aisles, as tightly wound as the prisoners. Something was going down. Something a lot bigger than any individual attack. But nobody seemed to know what that would be, or where it was going to come from.

♣

AFTER SUPPER, a group of Aryans positioned themselves to the far right of the shower room. A young white inmate walked toward them, a towel in his hand.

"Fish," one of the thugs hissed.

The young white man stepped to the other side, and found himself on black turf, where he was immediately accosted. "You in the wrong part of town, Chuck!"

The white inmate turned away, mumbling apologies, but too late—he found himself surrounded by blacks. The same whites who had been ready to rape the young man now moved in to defend him, chesting their way forward.

The distinct sound of a shell being jacked into a chamber chilled the entire shower room. All eyes turned to a trio of guards: one kneeling, two standing, all ready to fire their "non-lethal" weapons. This was a kill-trained team, eyes unreadable behind their face shields, but there was no mistaking their orders.

"Better come with us," one of the whites said to the young man, putting his arm around the kid's shoulders.

"Thanks, man. I didn't know. . . ."

"It's okay," the older man told him, comfortingly.

As he walked the kid toward the right side of the shower room, two of his crew stayed behind, watching his back. And waiting their turn.

"Fresh meat," one said to the other.

"Yeah. Looks juicy, too," the other responded.

As the words left his mouth, a tiny line of darkness appeared to circle one of the showerheads, throbbing as if it had a pulse. At the word "meat," the circle became arrow-shaped, pointing down:

"Hit!"

♣

AT THE scream, the squad charged into the shower. They found one of the would-be rapists dead on the floor, his blood flowing into the drain. But even the most invasive search failed to turn up a weapon of any kind.

It wasn't until the bag-and-tag team took the required photos that the presence of a tattoo on the dead man was noted.

"Must be a new one," the camera operator said, looking at the jack of spades overlapping the ace of hearts.

By the time the body was wheeled into the infirmary, the tattoo had disappeared.

And the photos the team took never came out.

♣

THAT SAME evening, Cross was again having a smoke on the tier, leaning over to watch the activity below. He turned at Banner's approach, and they began a conversation.

Suddenly, the Riot Bell sounded. The goon squad thundered past, sweeping convicts out of its way like a bulldozer.

"Goddamn it!" Banner rasped out. "They must've made another move. This keeps up, we might as well have it go all-out."

♣

IN THE prison hospital unit, a white inmate was lying on a bed, the back of which was elevated to put it in something close to a sitting position. No injuries were visible, but his face was bleached out, as if his eyes had seen something too much for his mind.

He was surrounded. Not only by guards, but also by men in suits who must be Administration from the way the guards deferred to them.

One of the suits shook his head, and made a gesture. The others walked out with him, leaving the contingent of guards in place.

Within minutes, the suits walked through the corridor, grim-faced. They didn't stop until they reached the Director's office.

♣

"HE'S STICKING to his story?" a gray-haired man asked the others.

"That's right, Chief," one of the suits replied.

"What's *your* take on it?"

"I'm not sure, sir. The kid's not lying. Not intentionally, anyway. Far as he's concerned, some kind of creature just . . . materialized or something. Then it hacked four Brotherhood members into hunks of meat."

"You think . . . ?"

"I don't know *what* to think. Those cons—the dead ones—they're known booty bandits. No question what they had on *their* minds when they muscled that kid into that corner—we even found a little tube of Vaseline on the floor. So, if it wasn't for the physical evidence, I'd say the kid was flying on chemicals and he just hallucinated the whole mess. Hell, that's what we've got him here for, right? Dope fiend?"

The suit looked up, his face grave. "He didn't hallucinate those bodies. *God!* They were done the same way Towers was. Like there's a goddamned *recipe* or something. And nobody saw a thing.

"Yeah, I know: in a place like this, nobody ever does. But this much is for real. Not even our own CIs know anything. And, with what we put on the table for them, they'd spill in a minute if they did."

♣

RUMORS WHIPPED like a vicious wind, gusting throughout the prison on razor wings, passing from whisperer to whisperer, each time picking up speed and adding content.

"They got four of our guys!" Banner said to Cross. "Four! This is out of control."

"*Now* you know why I'm here?" Cross asked.

"Yeah. And all glory to Odin that you are. I've got over twenty calendars in, and I've never seen anything like it. Even when they had us outnumbered five to one, they couldn't make things like *this* happen."

"I'm gonna need some stuff. . . ."

"Whatever it is, you got it," Banner promised, as solemnly as a new bride.

♣

VISITING DAY. Tiger waited patiently in line for her pass. She was dressed in a burnished-gold short-sleeved T-shirt several sizes too small, black spandex pants, and bronze spike heels with black soles. Nobody was looking anywhere else: male or female, black or white, convict or guard.

"Prison's prison, but that there is just plain wrong," a black convict whispered to the man next to him as Tiger strutted past. "I knew there was still women out there, but this is downright ridiculous, bro. How am I supposed to look my wife in the eye, now? That woman could *always* tell when I was slip-sliding around. Now I'm in a place where she knows I can't be getting any pussy. But I bet I got that exact same look on my face, right this minute."

Tiger greeted Cross with a deep kiss and tight embrace. Her mouth stayed locked on his a long time. If the guard hadn't been busy gaping at the wonder of spandex, he might have told them to break it off.

The Visiting Room was as racially divided as the rest of the prison. Cross escorted Tiger over to a corner, a move requiring them to walk the entire length of the room. Cross looked neither left nor right. Physical attacks can happen anyplace in a prison, but the Visiting Room was considered sacrosanct space—*any* excuse to cancel visiting privileges would be a victory for the guards and a defeat to all prisoners, regardless of color.

Cross slid into an empty space created by Brotherhood members. He sat with his back to the wall, virtually disappearing behind a human curtain.

On the other side of the large room, a young man who was once "Roscoe" from a disguised posse car spoke respectfully to a man known to him. Not personally, but as a trusted comrade of his own leader.

Roscoe left his gangbanger threads at home. He was dressed in a neat business suit, talking to a middle-aged black man wearing a tricolor African knit cap.

The man was one of obvious importance, as could be judged from the phalanx of on-the-alert convicts surrounding him on all sides. He was deep in conversation with Roscoe when Cross and Tiger walked by. Not a flicker of recognition showed on either man's face.

Cross took Tiger's hand, pulled her into the corner with him. His eyes danced over the room as they spoke softly to each other. After a few minutes passed, he got up and approached a white guard.

Over the guard's shoulder were the restrooms. Though they were once painted MEN and WOMEN, that paint had long since been worn off. And never replaced. It was common knowledge that the left room was for contraband transfer, the right one for sex. Only one couple at a time was allowed in either.

"You're next," the guard told Cross.

As a man and woman emerged from the restroom, arms around each other, Cross again took Tiger's hand and walked her with him to the vacated spot.

Inside, he leaned against her, speaking only for her ear.

"They're here," Cross said. "No question. Got four more last night."

"Save some for me," Tiger answered, pulling her T-shirt up to her neck. Cross pressed her against the wall. The surveillance camera captured the groping, but not the mouth-to-mouth transfer, an exact duplicate of the "greeting" kiss they had used to test that same system earlier.

♣

JUST WHAT was transferred was not known until Cross had passed through three separate search stations before being allowed back to his cell.

Cross sat on his cot, smoking as if deep in thought, watching through veiled eyes. Suddenly, the entire wing was plunged into darkness. As the inmates cursed and the guards tried to fight off panic, Cross removed a wafer-thin micro-chip from behind the back molar where Tiger had planted it with the tip of her tongue. After many rehearsals, he was able to open the back of the prison-issued radio working by touch alone. It only took a few seconds to insert the microchip.

♣

BY THEN, Tiger was on her way out of the institution. But before she stepped off the grounds to enter the parking lot, she was cornered by a guard who clearly spent a lot of time in the weight room—a state-of-the-art facility installed to help prison employees deal with the stress of their jobs. Another "working-class union victory" in a country where the sala-ries of prison guards are triple those of child-protection caseworkers.

"You look like a smart girl," the guard leered, looming over Tiger. "I'll bet you know how you could make it real easy on your man back there." As if accidentally, his finger-tips lightly brushed across her breasts.

"Really? How?" Tiger asked, wide-eyed and smiling sweetly.

"It's easy. You *go* along; he *gets* along, see? You like to play games, honey?"

"I *love* to play games," Tiger purred.

"Yeah? What's your favorite?"

"Squash," Tiger whispered, her lips twisting from come-hither to combat-snarl. The guard, instantly paralyzed and about to faint from the stabbing pain, futilely tried to pry her vise grip off his testicles—so recently engorged, but now in danger of withdrawing completely into his body.

As the guard slumped to the ground, still cupping his sack and mewling, Tiger walked off, her spike heels clicking a challenge to anyone else with bad ideas.

♣

THE NEXT morning, the surveillance cameras planted throughout the prison flashed various war-zone images. Roving gangs stalked the corridors, armed with a variety of homemade weapons. The level of organization was impressively military: one man walked point, the next men up carried the heaviest weaponry, the last man walked backward.

Even as the convict patrols were in motion, other prisoners were working on rearmament: carefully turning out shanks from any material possible, sharpening them down to needle points, wrapping their handles in tape.

Specialists were at work as well. One was twirling a glue-coated piece of rope through a pile of finely ground glass; another was fashioning a crude zip gun out of a length of tubing, a carved-wood pistol stock, and a thick rubber band for the nail that would serve as a firing pin.

"We only got two bullets," the con keeping watch said to the gun-builder, opening his hand to show the tiny cartridges within, "and they're .22 shorts. Tell the Sandman he's got to be *close*."

Some convicts were walking alone. One moved stiffly—the steel bar stolen from the weight room and now hidden down the leg of his pants hampering his movements. Another apparently unarmed warrior's entire upper body was wrapped in "Convict Kevlar"—thick layers of dampened newspaper.

On the yard, a group of blacks practiced a complex set of martial-arts katas under the watchful eye of their instructor. The Aryans were neither planning nor practicing, they were already picking out potential targets. A lone Latino squatted as far away from the black and white crews as possible. He was delicately fingering a short length of razor wire, heavily tape-wrapped at one end.

♣

WITHIN MINUTES, any illusion of organization had disappeared. Close combat raged over every screen.

One camera showed a black man cornered by a group of whites. He held a two-pointed shank in one hand, poised to strike, but it was obvious he wasn't going to survive the coming encounter.

Another showed a white convict taken out from behind by a pipe-wielding black.

The cameras were capable of zooming when hand-operated. Usually set to "automatic sweep," now they were individually manned. A close-up showed a dark hand holding a small glass bottle with a rag wick. He lit the wick and threw the bottle into a cell, which exploded in flames. The camera did not reveal how the unseen firebomber had managed to get inside the Isolation Wing.

"Tell my Juanita I died a man . . ." one Latino murmured to his crew as they dragged him from a battle scene, his life bleeding away from multiple stab wounds.

A slim but hard-muscled Latino wearing a T-shirt knotted at the midriff over a pair of bleached jeans with the back pockets removed whirled in mid-stride, a curved piece of honed steel in his hand. "Come on!" he challenged an unseen menace. "I got what you want right here, don't I? So come and take it, *puta*. You call me *maricón? Bueno. Quién es más macho, eh, puerco?*"

♣

THE IIT—the prison's Internal Investigation Team—was standing outside a large cell, clad in full-body armor. One was shining a high-intensity lamp, the other taking photographs. They paid no attention to the large group of black convicts in the background, perhaps because five other members of their team were facing that direction, their hands full of firearms which clearly failed to meet any "non-lethal" criteria.

Two fresh kills were hanging inside. Neither had a spinal cord; only one had even a fragmentary piece of a skull.

"Twenty-nine, documented," the cameraman said.

"Damn! They've never hit in this wing before," the man shining the light replied.

"Who knows?" The cameraman shrugged off the statement. "The pictures I take never come out anyway."

♣

BACK IN the Administration office, the IIT leader was making his report. "Chief, they took out a few more. Must have been *before* the riot jumped off. Same as in the shower room. Four men were in the rec cell at the end of the corridor. Playing cards, far as we can tell. All blacks. Probably UBG.

"Why they let this guy Camden live, we don't know. We don't have him registered as UBG, but we know he rolled with them. Still, he wasn't a member. Never inked up, either."

A studious-looking member of the IIT was holding a file in his hand. "I'll tell you what was different about that one, Chief. He didn't do it."

"Do what?"

"The crime. Yes, I know, the whole joint's full of innocent men. But it really looks like this guy Camden was outright railroaded. He was just a kid when he first came into the system—crime committed on federal property, some park, I guess. They probably only sent him here to send a message to blacks on the street. There's *nothing* in his file that connects him to that rape he's doing time for."

"I don't know his case, just his charges. What are you saying, the whole thing never happened?"

"No, the girl was gang-raped, all right. And they got the guys who did it. Five of them, matter of fact. This guy Camden, like I said, he was just a kid at the time. He *was* hanging out with the men who committed that rape, but that was much earlier that day, a good nine hours before the rape went down.

"And get this: the woman herself—the *victim*—she even said as much during the trial. Pointed right at Camden and said he *wasn't* one of the ones who raped her."

"And he was *still* convicted?"

"I guess he was, although I'm damned if I can see how. No fingerprints, no DNA, solid alibi. This is one kid who never got a break."

"He sure got one last night," the Chief said, turning to address the entire IIT. "This has got to stop. I need all the shot-callers in here. And I mean now!"

♣

INSIDE THE conference room. At one end was the Chief, flanked by openly armed guards. At the other end: Banner, the middle-aged black man in the tricolor cap, and a Latino with three tears prominently tattooed on the right side of his face, just below his eye.

The Chief addressed all the convicts collectively. "This is how it's going to be, from now on. I brought you men in here because the killings have to stop. They *don't* stop, and I'd just as soon have you all gunned down.

"Now, you all know I can do that. Another escape attempt gone wrong, who'd be shocked at that? And there wouldn't be any of that 'At-ti-ca' bullshit, not this time. You *must* know we've got every one of your crews infiltrated. And that the security cameras see only what we *want* them to see."

"You can't fake—"

"Can't fake *what*, Banner? Can't fake a convict we *own* stabbing a guard? Why even fake it? And why would we miss a guard who was bringing in drugs . . . or maybe even pistol that ended up in another convict's hand. You know, that same convict who *started* the whole escape attempt."

"I believe you," the black man said. "You people got Freon for blood."

"You're not wrong, Nyati. And I'd rather go that route than put up with *anything* that makes it looks like I can't control my own house. If this is some stupid game to get the media on your side, it's already failed."

His eyes still on the black man, the Chief continued: "We're telling nothing but the truth in here today. I'll be dead-center straight. Nyati, at first we thought this was your gang's work. It looked like one of your typical UBG moves. But now some of your own men have been hit, and in exactly the same way.

"And you, Ortega, maybe you thought your *carnales* could lay back, let the other colors cut their numbers. But when Montero and Rodriguez got done the same way, you knew you were in the kill-zone, too. There's only one color that counts in here anymore. That's red. Blood red.

"Banner, your guys took the whole first wave of hits—which was why we had it down to Nyati's crew—but you're not who we want, either. You might just be cold enough to sacrifice a few of your own crew if they were worthless to you—especially if they were working both sides; I already admitted that's what *we'd* do, right? But you don't have what you'd need to make *this* kind of bloodbath."

The Chief fired up his pipe, taking his time about

it, emphasizing who was ultimately in charge. Then he launched into his prepared speech:

"Like I said, I'm being straight with you. With you *all*, and all at the same time. Why? Because I don't want any garbage floating around the rumor mill. This way, if one man lies about what went on here today, the other two can call him on it.

"But this next part's even more important: I don't want *anyone* to think one of you is holding more cards than the other. I know there's no such thing as equality—not in here, not out in the World. You can say 'gangs' or you can say 'countries,' no real difference. But one side's *always* got the edge, and I can't have convicts believing *any* gang has got more firepower than I can call up."

The three gang leaders stood erect, arms folded in front of their chests, nothing showing on their faces. They knew the fact that they weren't cuffed had been no gesture of respect—it was the warden's naked display of power.

"I don't care who started it, or why. But if there's any more damn killing of any kind, this whole place goes on lockdown," the Chief said, the very lack of inflection in his voice underscoring that this was no idle threat; it was a guarantee.

The Chief hand-gestured the three men to come closer to his desk. The guards parted to clear a space for them, then closed in behind. On either side of the Chief's desk, the guard had been smoothly replaced by a man in a balaclava, holding a pistol in two hands, elbows braced against each body-armored chest.

Both men's eyes had that soft, wet look any convict knew. If any of the gang bosses so much as leaned in the Chief's direction, all three were chopped meat.

"Now, listen, and listen good," the Chief told them, his voice both quiet and hard. "I didn't say what I'm about to say, understand? Nobody here is ever going to *say* I did. The cameras are on, but that's just in case any of you want to play kamikaze. You never heard straighter talk from my side of the fence, and you never will.

"Okay, listen up. You think we don't know about the dope coming in? Or the gambling, the loan-sharking, the pimping? *Any* of the rackets your crews run? You think we *haven't* broken the codes in your letters? Listened in on your three-way calls? You don't think we've got informers all over the place?

"But have we keep-locked any of you? No. Any other joint in the country, you'd all be in black-hole Ad Seg. In fact," he said, pausing a little to let his words sink in, "you've all been wondering when we're going to get around to that.

"Well, we were never *going* to. We've been letting you guys run your own rackets for a long time, haven't we? You think we don't know which officers are on your payrolls? There's things you can't use your own mules for—we know all about that. And the cell phones, too.

"But you couldn't stand prosperity, could you? You had to go and break the contract. Some of your guys have done some nasty stuff. Okay, we know there's always going to be a certain amount of killing inside a place like this. It happens. But not the way it's happening now."

The Chief puffed on his pipe a couple of times before he spoke again.

"That contract between us didn't have to be signed for everyone to know what was on the paper. You get a whole lot of . . . privileges, let's call them, and I get a nice, quiet joint. Not so quiet that it would make anyone watching suspicious, but *under control*. I lose that, *you* lose it all.

"We know you've got some of the tunnel system mapped. After lights-out, you've been doing whatever you want down there. Every crew's got its own section, and nobody's been stupid enough to make *us* carry a body upstairs to the blocks.

"So listen close. We've got enough space in the black-out rooms for all of you—not just the shot-callers, *all* of you. This is a federal institution, remember? So if space gets tight we can always use a little bus therapy to fix the problem.

"We can keep this whole place on lockdown for as long as it takes to break every racket, wreck every system, destroy every network—all the things you've invested years to build up.

"And if you make us go *that* far, we can even make a few bodies ourselves.

"By tomorrow, we'll have *double* staffing in place. Every new man is going to be on loan from a cell-extraction team— and you know who gets recruited for *that* kind of work.

"You ever try to live on one meal a day? Especially when you're afraid to breathe too deep with all the gas floating around?

"And that's just the beginning. The public is *not* going to do a damn thing for you. There isn't going to be any media sympathy. No little Web site is going to 'report' to the out-side. Cyber-troops can't do anything but post a bunch of silly crap anyway. Nobody's going to take them seriously.

"Why do you think we don't care about the cell phones? Even that piece of garbage Manson got his hands on one. Once it hit the papers, they had to take it away from that sick little freak. But nobody bothered *yours*, did they? Ever wonder why?

"That's all about to end unless this *stops*. So—anybody got anything they want to say?"

"It's not us," Nyati jumped in first. "When we thought this maniac was just snuffing Caucs, we didn't give a damn. But now that he did some of us, we want him as bad as you do."

"It wasn't any of my guys, either," Banner said. "Hell, how could we get a man into the nigger wing anyway? You got the cameras, so you *know* it wasn't us."

Ortega shrugged his shoulders expressively. "We are in the middle," he said. "Like always. And the killer has taken some of ours as well. Would we seek revenge? There is no choice—if we cannot protect our own, we are nothing. But we do not believe it was *any* prisoner doing all this."

"Nobody knows nothing, that's the way you want to play it?" the Chief said. "About what I expected. The problem is, I don't think you're playing. I truly believe you don't know one damn thing about what's been going down. But if I have to ask you again, and you *still* don't know the answer, I will."

♣

CROSS AND Tiger were inside one of the Visiting Room bathrooms. They stood derma-close, speaking at a level well below whispering.

"It's time to tell me the truth," Cross said. "All of it. Whoever's doing whatever's happening in here, it's not something I ever dealt with."

Tiger took a breath, then told Cross everything her team knew in one continuous rush, careful to separate provable fact from legend, myth, and rumor, but not leaving anything out.

Cross listened closely, taking it all in. Then he whispered back: "This . . . thing, it's not new. Been around since forever, like you said. Signature kills, but all over the globe, so it *can't* be any single one of . . . whatever the hell they are.

"No pictures. No forensics. And no survivor testimony, either. When they hit, whoever's around that they *don't* kill, those people never see anything. No game—they *actually* don't see anything.

"But I already might know something, something you might want to throw into those computers of yours. There was a three-man kill in here just a little while ago. All in the same crew. All blacks, all sitting together. One of them, guy named Camden, he wasn't *touched*. But he didn't *see* anything. And, you know what? I believe that.

"What a sucker you all turned me into, huh? None of you have ever managed to even *see* one of them, never mind kill one for the autopsy table. And I'm supposed to capture one *alive?*"

"That's what *Blondie* wants," Tiger corrected him. "He thinks interrogation is the only way we'll ever find out whoever they are. And why they're doing what they do."

"You trust him?"

"Get real. We all know his backup plan is not leaving witnesses. But he's the only way Tracker and I could get a shot at the vengeance we swore. We're outsiders . . . like you."

"Didn't you say there's a rumor that a couple of them *did* get killed?"

"Yeah, but, like I *also* said, we don't have any idea if it's true. There was a report out of Africa, claimed two of them took an anti-tank round dead-center, blew them into little pieces. But, whoever they are, they always come for their dead, and they come *fast*. All we have is that one radio transmission. By the time a team got to the spot, it was nothing but fried earth."

"What else?"

"They're hunters, that's all we *really* know. And they only seem to hunt hunters, if that makes any sense."

"Maybe it does. But I'm damned if I know what kind of sense it could make."

"I know. It's not like anyone was hunting *them*. All we can figure is that this is like what would have happened if some UFO dropped down and rescued the Roman gladiators. But it rescued them too late—the gladiators had too much blood in their mouths to spit it out, use a toothbrush, and start over again as regular people.

"It's not like they took a vote and decided fighting was more fun than farming. It's like they were . . . transformed into something. And killing, that's just . . . that's just what they *do*, you know?"

"You sound like you don't hate them."

"Why would I?" ·

"Then, if they just do it because that's what they are, why are you and Tracker going after them?"

"Because that's what *we* do," Tiger said.

Cross lit a cigarette. "They really came to the right place this time, huh? They want human-hunters, this joint's full of them."

"I know. We figure that's why they hit that serial-killer freak. . . ."

"Yeah . . ." Cross mused. Then snapped his fingers. "Maybe *that's* it."

"What?"

"There's been a couple of their kills in here. On the surface, they look the same as all the others. But on two of them, they let someone go, let them just walk away, like that Camden guy I told you about. They gave the same kind of pass to some white kid, too."

"Oh, both of them got interrogated, trust me," Tiger says. "Blondie pulled them right out of this place. But they don't even remember *being* where it happened, never mind seeing anything. And that squares with other stuff we have. Like doing their number on a whole safari, but letting the natives go. Still, even that much, it's only talk."

"The stuff in *here* wasn't talk," Cross told her. "That white kid was about to be raped. Camden, the black guy, I'm not sure what the deal with him was, but the grapevine says he's innocent, shouldn't even be here in the first place. And his charge *was* rape. How could this . . . thing tell if a man was innocent?"

"Maybe they can smell it or something," Tiger guessed. "Maybe that's why dogs can smell *them*, I don't know. But whatever they are, they're not animals. At least not any animal anyone's heard of. It's like they kill for some reason, only we don't know what that could be. Maybe it's a . . . game or something, like that big-bucks consultant told us. And if all they count are the hardest targets, what's harder than humans?"

"Yeah," Cross thought aloud. "But if a killer's kills belong to whoever kills *him*, maybe the goal was to get the highest body count."

"So killing a serial killer—?"

"You're sure it's set up with Nyati?" Cross cut her off. He knew that, even with greasing the guards, surveillance was extra-high, and the warning knock on the door was going to come soon.

"Yes. But confirm over the transmitter first."

"Sure. But tell your team there isn't a whole lot of time left. Whoever they are, *what*ever they are, they've been going through this joint like pigs on pie."

♣

NIGHT FOUND Cross lying on his bunk, eyes closed, the earplug from his institutional radio inserted. Not an uncommon sight: a lot of cons used their radios as noise-blockers to let them sleep.

Behind his eyelids, Cross watched the limousine carrying the toadish man drive away. And saw the explosion that followed. His mind was working the logic string, doing the death-math.

Maybe they were there. Right in the middle of the blast. If that's true, we can't kill them no matter what we use. You can't kill "kill." But if they can get . . . splattered, maybe they have to reassemble before they can work again.

Cross nodded, as if something he suspected had just been verified. He pulled the earplug free and got to his feet. Silently, he twisted the heel off one shoe and removed the wire inside, working in complete darkness.

At the wire's end was a tiny bulb. A closer look would have revealed that the wire itself was divided into several sections, each one no more than a few inches long.

Cross wrapped individual pieces of wire around the base and top of each of the bars in his cell window. He then connected the ends of all the wires into the one anchored by the bulb. He squeezed the bulb and stepped back. A faint hissing sound accompanied the just-released acid as it ran through the hollow wires into the bars.

Less than a minute later, Cross pulled the still-smoking sections of bars away from his cell window. He opened a carton of cigarettes and removed packages of dental floss braided into a thick strand. From the heel of his other shoe, he removed a center-weighted, tri-barbed plastic hook, folded flat. Released from the pressure that had kept it folded, the hook opened fully.

Cross tied one end of the braided floss around his waist, and looped the other around the chain holding his bunk to the wall. Then he reached out the window, supported himself with one hand, and used the other to fling the weighted hook up over his head. It took four attempts before he could feel the hook lock solidly into place.

His next step was to put on his shoes. Pulling at the side of each sole exposed another, much thinner one underneath. Those undersoles were coated with a sticky compound. Climbing gear, originally developed to give second-story men an edge, it had later been perfected by Buddha, to keep the crew ahead in the permanent arms race always running through the underworld.

Cross worked his way up, planting each sole securely, moving without haste. The rooftop was various shades of black: from the shadow-pools just past the rooftop to the faint glow from the surrounding lights, and the occasional penumbra from the bright swathe cut by tower searchlights.

Cross saw three figures, standing as if they had been waiting for him. He approached with deliberation, hands held away from his body in the universally understood gesture.

Two black men stepped forward. One carried a heavy shank, the other a much heavier lead pipe.

Cross put his hands up, stood still for their thorough search.

"Clean," one said.

Nyati stepped forward. "Take off your shirt," he said. "I want to see something for myself."

Cross obeyed. He didn't move as Nyati used a pencil flash to zero in on the tattoo. "Yeah. It's exactly like Butch described it."

Together the two men walked into a pool of total blackness, leaving the other two standing guard.

Nyati faced Cross. "I told Butch I'd meet with you. One time. There ain't gonna be no more, so say *everything* you got to say."

"These killings, easy enough to say they're all about color, but we both know that's not what's going on."

"We do, huh?"

"You know damn well I'm telling the truth. The UBG hasn't got anybody who can walk through walls, and neither does the Brotherhood. It's not *lobos*, either. There's a hunter loose in this joint, and he's working the place like a wolf turned loose in a corral of sheep. A concrete corral, with chained-up sheep."

"You know who he is?"

"I don't even know *what* he is . . . but he's not one of us."

"He's not white?"

"He's not *human*. Not anymore, anyway. He's a trophy-taker, and his tribe is keeping score. Under their system, you kill a killer, you get credit for all *his* kills."

"I'd say you was crazy," Nyati replied, "except I saw some of the bodies myself. What the hell they want with spines and skulls anyway?"

"I don't know. It's their mark, the one they always leave behind. Like fang-and-claw marks you see in the jungle. A signature kill."

"How you figure on stopping something like that? Specially in here, with no guns?"

"Guns wouldn't do it. *If* there's a way, it's gotta be slice, not shoot. But maybe there *is* a way. I say 'maybe' because the odds don't look good. But to even give us *that* much of a chance, you gotta work with me."

"I only work with my own kind."

"Look, I'm not doing the 'some of my best friends are black' number, and there's no time for that cred crap anyway. If Butch hadn't gotten word to you, why would you be up on this roof right now?

"All you need to know—I guess I should say *believe*—is that, in this war, I *am* your own kind. Long as that . . . thing's around here, the *human* race is the only race that counts.

"It's always some kind of 'us against them,' right? Black against white, outlaws against citizens. But there's one thing I learned a long time ago—no warrior is stronger than War. Until whatever that thing is goes down, we're all the same color, just different shades."

"So what are those people—"

"That's just it. They're not 'people' at all. So when I say it's us against them, that's just what I mean."

Cross pulled a pack of cigarettes from his shirt pocket. Without offering a smoke to Nyati, he fired it up, cupping the end with both hands.

"You know why I'm here," he said. "And *I* know you got that word from people you trust. So do whatever you have to do, talk it over with whoever you need to. Make a decision, and get word to me."

"How?"

"Friday, at noon mess, I'm gonna step into No Man's Land. Alone. If you're with me, you step into it, too. Make sure your men stand down. I'll do the same. And then I'll tell you how we can pull it off. *Maybe* pull it off. I'll tell you face to face, right there."

Nyati looked at Cross. "You ain't short on balls, I'll give you that."

Cross slowly turned around and walked away, not looking back. The three black men were deep in conversation as Cross slipped over the rooftop and lowered himself back into his cell.

As he pulled the bars back into their original position and coated the broken spots with a black substance that gave off a faint hissing sound, a long, thin shadow shape-shifted on the roof.

The words "No Man's Land" vibrated. Then, from inside one of the bars Cross had just sealed:

"Stay. . . ."

Two corners of torn playing cards trembled in the light breeze: the ace of hearts, and the jack of clubs.

♣

"**I THINK** you're crazy," Tiger told Cross on Wednesday.

"You saying it won't work?"

"I'm saying we don't *know*. Nothing like what you're talk-ing about has ever been tried."

"Just because Wanda can't find it in her computers? I've been thinking about everything you told me. Doing time is good for that, thinking about the past. Roman gladiators that don't know how to farm . . . Maybe we're dealing with some kind of . . . presence. That's the best way I can put it. All these kills, all over the world, for so many years—it can't be some mob doing that."

"Because?"

"Because no gang survives that long without takeover attempts. Maybe there's a palace coup, like there was in Liberia. Maybe it's a street shooting, like outside Stark's Steakhouse in New York. Maybe it's spreading the word that someone's in custody . . . and cooperating. A million differ-ent ways. And nobody's ever tried *any* of them? Ever?

"And even if any gang could survive for centuries—hell, it would have to be a lot longer than that—what's in it for them *now*, all of a sudden?" Cross continued to answer Tiger's one-word question. "There's never been a ransom demand, never been a warn-off note; they never try to *occupy* territory. There's no money. There's only this . . . slaughter they do. And even that, it just doesn't feel like revenge."

"So what *does* it feel like?"

Cross held Tiger's dark-amber eyes, speaking very softly. "It feels like pain. It feels like when someone gets killed—I don't mean die of old age, or in combat—I mean . . ."

His voice stopped. He breathed slowly through his nose, trying to self-center, knowing he wouldn't get another chance.

"Okay, this may sound crazy to you, but it's all I've got. I'm not sure, but . . . maybe when someone gets killed for someone else's fun, maybe their pain doesn't die with them."

"That's nice poetry. What are we supposed to do with it?"

"Look, I don't think it matters where they come from. All we know is that there's certain work they do. And whatever *that* is, it always ends up in enough spine-ripped hanging corpses to make its own forest."

"So you couldn't get close to—?"

"It's not something I'd *want* to get close to. But I know something that might take one of them down, keep him nice and quiet until you can come and get him. And I got the perfect damn place to do it. Right here. Now, all you have to do is *listen*," he whispered.

Tiger remained silent for several minutes. Her only response was "Cross . . ."

"Can you get it for me? Yes or no?"

"Sure. It's no big deal. We got real small ones now."

"I need three of them."

"Three?! What could you possibly—?"

"Don't worry about it. Just remember: three of them, fast as you can, okay?"

"Okay," Tiger agreed, her eyes sorrowful.

"What're you so sad about?" Cross asked her. "No matter if I'm right or wrong, you'll be outside the blast zone."

"Are *all* men stupid?" Tiger said. Her face softened for a brief second, then hardened into a warrior's mask.

She turned to leave, then felt Cross's hand on her shoulder.

"What?"

"Can I ask you a question?"

"Sure." She shrugged.

"Why does Percy think you're a dyke?"

"Percy thinks any woman who's not interested in him is such a rare phenomenon that it can only be explained by her being a lesbian. Truth is, I'm bi. What difference could that make?"

"Sure, I get that much. But the blond guy, too. And Wanda—"

"Those two are bloodless robots. But they're not the same kind of robot. I could stick my boobs in Blondie's face and he wouldn't even blush. But if I so much as come *near* Wanda, she gets feelings she doesn't want to have."

"I get it."

"Get what?"

"Why you and Tracker can work with people like them. It's your only way in, isn't it?"

"Until now," Tiger said, and she spun around and walked away, transfixing those watching in the process. Hers was a purposeful move—not a single eye in the room turned toward Cross.

♣

CROSS SAT next to Banner at the mess table. His mouth barely moved, but his body posture was so intense and urgent that other members moved as far away as possible without leaving their posts.

Finally, Cross stood up. Slowly and deliberately, he walked into the traditional No Man's Land of cleared space between whites and blacks. A guard started to step forward but stopped in his tracks as Nyati arose from his crew's table and moved toward Cross.

The entire mess hall was silent. Dead silent. The guards froze, knowing that if a full-scale race war jumped off in that enclosed space, they weren't going to make it out alive.

When Cross and Nyati were close enough to bump noses, Cross started to speak, his words inaudible to all but the leader of the UBG. When he finished, he stepped back an inch.

Then he said, still under his breath, "If you buy it, there's nothing else for me to say. I just told you all I know. For this one, it *is* us against them. You believe that, then it's the Death House. Bring whatever you want, bring *who*ever you want. But it's only going to be the five of us doing the actual work. That means we *all* lose some men."

"All?"

"All," Cross confirmed. "Human body armor isn't going to keep them off for long. If they get to us before we're ready, we're done, too."

"Five? You and me, that leaves three short."

"Ortega and Banner."

"Banner? That Nazi's already been breathing longer than he should. What do we need with *two* white men?"

"Who's the boss of the Hmongs?"

"Recognized them right away, huh? They a seriously bad bunch, man. But that crew, it's also got Vietnamese, Chinese, Japanese . . . probably others I don't even know about. And, listen now, in *here*, they forget all that. They play it like an all-for-one mob. They got no choice. But you can see they really don't like each other any more than they do us."

"It's only the Hmong guy I want."

"Why him?"

"I speak a few words of the language. I can break it down for him."

Nyati stared hard at Cross. And took the same in return.

"Okay, man. It's your show. What time?"

"Midnight."

"Done."

"For the race!" Cross shouted. But before anyone on either side could react, Nyati echoed, "For the race!"

Then, to the stunned surprise of all watching, they stood in the middle of No Man's Land, and clasped hands.

♣

MIDNIGHT. THE Death House area was clogged with convicts, still divided along racial lines, but not openly antagonistic toward one another. Frightened would be a better description of their mood, fear was the single unifying factor among them.

Whites, blacks, and Latinos were all there, even a sprinkling of Asians. Everyone was armed with whatever they were able to procure from the broad spectrum of prison-available weapons.

Men just before combat act the same way in prison as they do on any battlefield: some smoke, some pace, some pray. Every man was anxious to get it on, and even more anxious for it to be over.

Cross was standing with Nyati and Ortega, their backs against the gas-chamber wall.

One of the Asians approached, a short, thin man holding what looked like a strip of razor blades on a string. His face could be that of a man anywhere between thirty-five and seventy-five, but his eyes were not those of a young man. Cross pointed to his right, confirming to Nyati that the Asian's appearance was not a surprise.

Banner detached himself from his crew and moved over to where the others were standing.

"Deal me in," he said.

"Just you?" Cross asked.

"Look around, brother. We're *all* here. But it's got to be me up front. I'm the shot-caller, so this is my place, too. Like you told me, this is for the race. So, whatever goes down, I'm down with it. But I have to go standing *up*, see?"

Cross nodded. He turned to Ortega. "Your man knows what to do?"

"For this, I *am* my man, *hermano*. After you first talked with me, I reached out. What you say, it is true. It has *always* been true. All the way back to the Aztecs. The Mayans and the Incas. So it is just like you and Nyati called it out. For the race!"

"For the race," Banner echoed, but very quietly.

Each man held up a fist, waist-high. And then they slammed them together in an unmistakable gesture of final unity.

♣

"**YOU SURE** it's coming, man?" Nyati asked.

"Look around you. If it wants to hunt the real life-takers inside these walls, we're the only game in town."

The Hmong nodded, but said nothing. Then he vanished.

♣

A TINY shadowy blotch materialized within the densely packed men. It thickened and lengthened, gathering mass. Then it began moving like an anaconda through a swamp. Blood spurted wildly as individual men were torn into random pieces. Their body parts flew through the darkness until they hit the nearest wall, where a stack of ripped-out spines began to pile up.

Some of the men tried to run, others stood their ground, desperately striking blindly at whatever was attacking them.

This had no effect on the presence, which continued to work its way over to where four men stood against the gas-chamber wall, two on each side of its door.

The darkness was filled with screams as body parts continued to fly. A red haze formed, so intense it seemed to attack the darkness itself.

Ortega slipped off to one side of the death chamber; Banner to the other. The Hmong was nowhere to be seen.

Cross and Nyati remained, now standing alone. At a "Go!" from Cross, they both stepped back through the opened door of the gas chamber, still watching the inexorable progress of . . . something as it moved through the wall of human flesh.

"Sweet Jesus!" Nyati muttered under his breath.

"Son of a bitch!" Cross said. "This is too soon. I was sure they'd—"

Cross cut himself off. The presence he felt to his right wasn't the one gutting and discarding individual prisoners; it was the Hmong, joining them.

The three men backed all the way into the chamber. Cross seated himself in the chair where condemned convicts were once strapped down. He lit a cigarette.

Nyati took the other chair—dual executions were far from uncommon in Chicago's past.

The Hmong crouched in a far corner, covered entirely in a dark mesh blanket.

A black mist approached the threshold of the death chamber. The men instantly realized the presence had been divided into small pieces by the slashing attacks of the mass of convicts it had oozed its way through. But then they all saw it begin to regroup into a unified mass.

Slowly, it struggled to form a single entity. The black blob had been deeply wounded—chunks of its border were missing, and gaping holes were visible within its remaining mass. And yet it kept moving forward, as if the human flesh it sought would be the replenishment it needed.

Just as the misty black mass entered the death chamber, Ortega and Banner slipped behind it and slammed the door closed. They dropped the heavy outside crossbar into place and took off, running.

They didn't run far. As soon as they reached the control room, both men randomly flipped a series of heavy switches, releasing cyanide pellets into a shallow pool of acid under the death chairs. A greenish gas immediately began to billow up.

"Now!" Cross yelled, reaching behind his neck and pulling a flat-faced mask with a dark filter over the front into place. Nyati and the Hmong did the same.

Cross jumped to his feet, drawing a heavy bear-claw knife from behind his back. Nyati unsheathed a thick length of pipe and waved his wrist; a razor-edged arrow popped free at each end. The Hmong cradled a beautifully crafted blowgun.

Without warning, Nyati and Cross attacked, slashing at the encroaching blackness . . . and finally penetrating the shadow-blob, which became more visible every time it took another hit.

The Hmong was the last to act. Holding the blowgun as a brain surgeon would a tumor-removal scalpel, he emptied his lungs to blast off a single shot.

The shadow collapsed, breaking into patches of black on the floor of the chamber. But the patches immediately began to pool once again.

Nyati crawled over to the mass, tentatively extending his hand.

"It's still alive. I can feel . . . something. Like a pulse, maybe. If we're gonna finish it—"

Cross pounded his palm hard against the door to the death chamber. Banner and Ortega threw off the crossbar and left it just long enough for the two men inside to dive out before they slammed it back home again. Neither of them realized that the Hmong had been the first to leave, gliding between Cross and Nyati.

Cross pulled off his mask, opened his mouth wide, reached in, and wrenched the phony molar free. He pressed the top of the tooth, which immediately began to hum.

"It's down. In the chamber," Cross said into the mini-mike, his voice calm, precise . . . and urgent.

♣

THE BLOND man was in the War Room, Wanda at his side. He was half-shouting into a fiber-stalk microphone. "All units. Go! Go! Go!"

Percy was behind the wheel of the unit's war wagon, cruising the highway closest to the prison. He picked up the blond man's message and stomped the gas pedal, hitting the red button on the dash that kicked in the twin turbo-chargers at the same time.

Tiger and Tracker were already in the shadow cast by the prison wall. They moved in from different directions.

Tiny black splotches began to reassemble inside the gas chamber. If the poison gas had any effect on this process, it was not apparent.

Adapting its shape to circumstances, the blackness flattened itself to micro-thinness. Then it slowly began to probe the seals of the death chamber's door, seeking an opening.

♣

NYATI, NEAR death, was trying to stand, using a wooden spear as a crutch. Banner stood with him, still slashing with a prison-built sword. But he, too, was fading fast.

Cross wasn't doing much better. He opened his eyes just as the chamber door began to crack at one of the top seals, pushed open by something blacker than darkness.

He had been expecting an Evac Team, but the blackness told him they were going to be too late. He sensed the shadow calling to whatever pieces outside the chamber were still unattached.

Calling them home.

Ortega and the Hmong attacked the thickening blackness from either side of the door, but their knife thrusts no longer had any effect.

Suddenly, the shadow-mass stopped writhing. A tiny

blue symbol glowed briefly on Cross's right cheekbone, just below the eye. As the blue mark crystallized into what would be a permanent scar, Cross plunged into unconsciousness.

♣

THE ONLINE edition of the *Chicago Tribune* screamed:

RACE WAR AT FEDERAL PRISON!
277 CONVICTS KILLED IN PRISON RIOT!
"WORST IN HISTORY" SAYS BUREAU OF PRISONS

"Tell me again, goddamn it!" the blond man said, almost incoherent with rage.

"By the time we got there, they were gone," Tiger repeated. "Maybe back to wherever they came from. The only trace they left behind was the body count."

"I'm done with this," Percy said. "Taking one alive, yeah, *that* was a brilliant idea. Look what it cost! And all for nothing."

"As long as I'm the head of this outfit, I don't give a damn *what* you think," the blond man responded, back to his bloodless self-control. "Get out of my sight, all of you. I've got to work up another capture scenario."

Except for Wanda, all the others walked away.

A soft gray shadow followed them briefly, as though to shield them from harm. After a moment, it started to flow in the other direction, back toward the blond man and Wanda. At above-human detection levels, the "capture scenario" line was repeated. Then . . .

"Hit!"

A glimmering pair of playing cards hovered over the heads of the blond man and Wanda: the ace and jack of clubs.

When the cards disappeared, the blond man and Wanda were hanging from the ceiling, missing their spines and skulls.

♣

"**THE OPERATION'S** been closed down," Tiger told Cross. They were in the Visiting Room, about a month after the "riot."

"Because Blondie and his girlfriend got done?"

"No. Although I can tell you, even Tracker got a little pale when we found them in the War Room, just . . . hanging like they were."

"The deal's still in place?"

"Immunity in front? I wouldn't bet the farm on it, not now."

"What *can* I get?"

"You can get out."

"I could do that without you. Remember, I'm not convicted of anything, and I've got a hunch the feds are going to drop the case."

"What *do* you want?"

"Stand up."

Cross held Tiger tenderly. As they kissed, his right hand dropped to Tiger's prominent butt. Every eye in the room followed that hand, not the one hidden under Tiger's thick, striped mane.

"I didn't think that would work," she said, speaking very softly.

"It was a mortal lock," Cross assured her. "There's a little scrap of paper under the back neckline of your sweater now. There's four names on it. They all need to have their cases reversed on appeal."

"So long as they didn't—"

"Four cases, three homicides, one rape. No kids, no drugs. And all innocent."

"That's still asking a lot. I don't mean from me—you know how they work."

"Yeah. Yeah, I do. But unless they handle this job, who're they going to debrief?"

"They don't need more than—"

"Yeah, they do. I think I've finally got this one figured out. And they'll need *all* of those guys on the list to have it make sense. Polygraph them, hit them with the truth serum, whatever they want. Maybe this time they'll go back and *actually* investigate. They'll see it for themselves."

"So you say."

Cross leaned in toward Tiger, his lips feather-touching her ear. "They didn't attack any of us—they . . . it . . . whatever it was, it only fought back in self-defense."

"They didn't hit me or Tracker, either. Percy's missing, but that could mean anything."

"Come back here and *listen*, okay? What I'm telling you is just between us. For now."

Tiger wiggled herself close, threw her left thigh over Cross's right. "How's this?"

"Very fine."

"Don't play games," Tiger warned him. "You think I had an orgasm when you grabbed my ass?"

"*I* came pretty damn close."

"Just stop! *Why* didn't they attack any of you?"

"I don't know. I mean, they kind of did. But what I *do* know is that they could have finished us if they wanted—we were all running on empty, blood included. So they're not kill-crazy; they were on a mission. It's got *something* to do with crime, but only certain kinds of crime."

"How can—?"

"Sssh! Just *listen*. It's like they're thinning the herd. Culling out the scum. You check the sheets of the men they slaughtered, I'll bet you find something in common."

"What?"

"I don't know. But it feels like . . . it feels like they're try-ing to . . . yeah, I know how *this* is gonna sound . . . like they're trying to take out the humans who're polluting their own race."

"But they're not—"

"Maybe not. But they kill humans, right? *That's* the race I'm talking about. We—humans, I'm saying—we're never satisfied with just killing each other, are we? No, we rape, we torture . . . we march people into gas chambers a lot bigger than the one we tried to trap *it* in. There's nothing you can do to a human being that hasn't *been* done. By other humans.

"That . . . shadow or whatever it was . . . it's like it was playing a game of blackjack. Only 'hit' doesn't mean 'hit *me*'— it means 'hit *them*.'"

"They can read the cards every person's holding?"

"Maybe it *is* something like that. The closest I can get to what I'm trying to say is . . . remember, when the Nazis marched people into the gas chambers, it wasn't just Jews. Homosexuals, Gypsies . . . it would have been everyone on the planet but themselves. And even *that* wouldn't have lasted."

"I know."

"No, you don't. That's the political part, not the . . . genetic, I guess. There's only one way to keep blood 'pure.' Inbreeding. And we know what happens in these families where incest covers too many generations. There's records going all the way back to Sawney Bean. And that's just *writ-ten* records. It might take us a while, but, eventually, the human race was going to rot from the inside out."

"I . . . I can see that. But the Nazis *didn't* succeed."

Cross took Tiger's hand in his. She made no move to pull away.

"Tiger, if you want to file this under 'Lunatic,' that's up to you. But what my mind keeps seeing is that smoke. The smoke from their ovens. That gray, shadowy smoke.

"What if, every time human slaughter ever occurred in the history of the world, there was *more* of that smoke? What if the smoke had . . . I don't know . . . something of the slaughtered people in it? What if it became a thing of its own?"

"I'm not telling those junior G-men any story like that."

"I don't want you to. *I'm* not telling them myself. I'll just feed them enough to send them alien-hunting."

"This . . . theory of yours, you want to keep it to yourself?"

"No, girl. If I'm wrong, we all go back to our lives, whatever they were before this. But if I'm right . . . I don't know how to say this, exactly. You know who I am; you know what I do. I'm not one of the good guys, and that was my choice.

"But if a hard rain's coming—if the filth is being washed out of our race—then, whoever they are, this is one job I *want* them to pull off."

Tiger looked deeply into Cross's eyes for a long moment. "Me, too," she finally said. "And when you get out, we have things to say to each other."

"How do I find you?"

"You just keep on working out of that Red 71 dump of yours, Mr. Cross. I'll find you."

♣

AS TIGER spoke, the graffiti-style red arrow leading to the basement poolroom began to work its way downstairs, looking much like an MRI of a boa constrictor swallowing its prey. In a language no human could understand, spoken at a pitch outside of human hearing range:

"Find you . . ."

And, just as nobody hears those words, nobody hears: "Stay!"

And nobody sees the quick flash of a river of aces and jacks spilling out of the bottom arrow, as if sprayed from the hose of a short, squat container of pesticide.

EPILOGUE

FOUR YEARS later . . .

♣

"**HEY, BUDDHA,** you seen Princess?" Rhino asked, his nearly five-hundred-pound body visually enlarged by the gray jumpsuit he habitually wore. The overall effect was to make the back door of the poolroom behind him seem non-existent. "He didn't come back to the spot last night."

"Maybe he got lucky," the short, pudgy man offered, glancing up from a white sheet of oilskin he had spread out on a desk made from a solid-core door positioned over a pair of sawhorses. On the cloth he had arranged various parts of an automatic pistol next to a micro-tool kit any surgeon would have envied. For illumination, three parallel tubes of the sunlight-replicator used to treat seasonal affective disorder hung overhead. "Even a full-bore maniac like him has to score once in a while. Law of averages."

"What's your problem with Princess anyway?" the giant demanded. "He doesn't mean any harm—you know that."

"He's like a little kid, Rhino," the pudgy man said, in a

"How many times do I have to say it?" tone. "A little kid, playing games. I'm a professional—so are you. Fact is, I can't figure out why Cross puts up with—"

"You want to know, why don't you ask him?" the giant responded. His voice was an incongruous high-pitched squeak, but to those who knew him, no less threatening than the grunting of a flotilla of angry alligators.

"Take it easy," Buddha said hastily. "What're you so worried about? This can't be the first time Princess didn't show."

"Yeah, it is," the huge man replied. "At least, he always left word."

"Hey, he's a grown man," Buddha said, suddenly turning gentle as he saw the genuine anxiety on his partner's face.

"No," Rhino replied, shaking his head sadly, "you're right—he's a big kid." The giant glanced quickly around the room. "Cross around somewhere?"

"He's always around somewhere," Buddha said, not a hint of interest in his voice. "Either he's up on the roof playing with those stupid birds of his, or else he's down at the Double-X checking out the new shipment."

"I'll go look," Rhino said. "Maybe he—"

"You're on duty, right?" Buddha told him, his voice softening again. "What if someone comes around? Me, I'm not doing nothing—just modifying the counter-balance on this piece. Let me go see if I can scare him up."

"Thanks, Buddha," Rhino said gratefully, a lower-register note of surprise in his usual squeak. He backed out the door and took up his post again.

Buddha quickly reassembled the pistol, slipped it into a shoulder holster, buttoned his charcoal-dyed field jacket, and exited through another door.

♣

BUDDHA TOOK the back staircase, then used a key to open a heavily braced steel door. The floors he passed had all been empty, as expected.

He made his way to the roof, musing that being the registered owner of several pieces of property didn't amount to an actual cash flow . . . as his wife constantly reminded him.

"You need make more money!" was her endless refrain, as if her shrill voice was on some permanent loop of unbreakable tape.

"How much more damn money could you possibly spend, So Long?" was Buddha's tired retort, memorized from constant repetition.

"You watch," she would say.

And proceed to prove her point. Again and again.

I don't know why I do it, Buddha thought to himself. Meaning, why go home at all? He was no stranger to shrewish women, but So Long made them all look like geishas. He could just walk away, find another place to sleep.

I can just hear Cross now, Buddha thought. *She knows too much.* He knew the gang leader's solution to any such potential problem would be a lethal one.

So what do I care?

Buddha could never answer that question, despite endless attempts. Introspection wasn't one of his skills.

♣

BUDDHA OPENED the door to the roof and stepped out gingerly. He scanned the terrain, his eyes sweeping over a lengthy wooden box that looked as if it had been carelessly discarded. He moved carefully, approaching the box the same way he had walked jungle trails years ago, always alert for trip wires.

A bird's head popped up from the center of the box, its

yellow-orange eyes gleaming with malevolence. "Don't get all excited," Buddha said softly. "I'm not messing with you—I'm just looking for Cross."

The bird's eyes tracked Buddha's every movement. It fluttered its wings briefly, as though considering flight. Buddha registered the flash of blue on the wings, confirming this was the male of the mated pair of kestrels that Cross maintained on the roof. Kestrels are small birds, less than a foot in total length, even including their long, stabilizing tail feathers, but they are fierce, relentless dive-bombers.

Much larger birds run for cover when a kestrel's shadow darkens the sky. The hunter-killers are blessed with incredible eyesight, awesome dive-speed, and deadly accuracy—the "one shot, one kill" snipers of the avian world.

Satisfied that Cross wasn't on the roof, Buddha carefully backed up until he was on the stairs. He gently closed the overhead hatch after him.

♣

THE LIVE GIRLS! sign on the Double-X flashed its blood-red neon against blacked-out window glass. Buddha opened the door, grateful for the sudden blast of air conditioning.

The doorman greeted Buddha by nodding his head a couple of inches. He knew better than to demand the cover charge—Buddha was the nominal owner of the joint. "We need a place where we can meet with people—a place we can control," Cross had argued.

"You got a thing for pole dancers, that's your problem," Buddha had responded. "How come *we* gotta chip in?"

"It could be a real moneymaker," Cross said.

"I don't know anything about running a strip joint," Rhino squeaked. "I'd rather do what we do. What we all do."

"I can get someone to run it," Cross said, thoughtfully.

"Tell you what . . . if it's not making money in six months, I'll buy out all your shares. Deal?"

Cross then turned to the rest of the crew, opening his hands at his sides to indicate he was ready to listen if anyone else had objections.

Ace pointed a finger at Cross, then at himself. He didn't need to say more—the two men had been partners since they were kids. Children too young for prison, but old enough to be incarcerated in one of the "training schools" that made Illinois nationally infamous.

"Come on, Rhino. It'd be fun," Princess had begged.

The giant reluctantly agreed, shaking his head at what he was sure was his own stupidity.

But after a rocky start, the joint was *coining* money. It always attracted the best girls, but not necessarily the most accommodating ones; its furnishings were decent, but hardly worthy of a sultan; and its cover charge was a ridiculously high fifty bucks. But what the club *did* have was some features not offered anywhere else in Chicago.

Word got around fast—if you danced at the Double-X, you never had to worry about the patrons getting out of hand. You didn't have to put out for the "manager," and if you didn't want to turn tricks—just strip and "dance"—that was okay, too.

Best of all, if you were having trouble with your boyfriend, the club instantly transformed itself into the world's only domestic-violence shelter for strippers.

"He started it!" Princess once said, explaining to the others why he had fatally fractured the skull of a low-level pimp who had slapped his one-girl stable. "He slapped Marisa, so I just slapped him back."

The pimp had noted Princess's hyper-muscled body—it was impossible to ignore—but had overlooked the physique because of its packaging: Princess had been wearing his usual rouge, eyeliner, and lipstick, highlighting his chartreuse tank top. In fact, he had been discussing makeup complexities with two of the dancers when the pimp had just walked into the dressing room.

Why Princess dressed so outrageously—and camped it up at every opportunity—was known only to a few. In his deranged mind, he could only act when another individual "started it." This brain-wave malfunction developed from his teen years, spent as a cage fighter in the headquarters of a Central American drug lord. Because he had been taken as a child, and fought so viciously that even his captors had been impressed, he was trained as a modern-day gladiator. After that training, he was kept for the amusement of those who enjoyed watching two men go at each other like bull elephants in mating season.

But Princess never wanted to fight—he wanted to make friends. Each and every time his opponent was led into the cage, Princess would ask if they couldn't be friends instead of fighting. When his offer was sneered at—and followed by an attack of some kind—Princess absorbed disappointment after disappointment until his mind finally developed the "He started it!" implant.

After he was pulled from the jungle by Rhino—who never explained why, and was never asked—Princess quickly realized that getting into fights was a lot more difficult when his opponent actually had a choice. Thus, the outrageously overdone presentation evolved. Another thing Princess had learned was that far too many tough guys actually believed homosexuals wouldn't fight.

The other man—or men; it made no difference to the muscle-armored terror—had to "start it." But once that fuse was lit, Princess could pull any adversary apart as easily as a loaf of fresh-baked bread.

♣

RHINO ALSO worked the floor sporadically—protecting his investment, he claimed. But it was an open secret that he stayed close in case Princess's protective instincts went too far.

Bruno, the man who worked the door, had a reputation of his own. He was a notorious life-taker who'd already served two terms: one for grievous bodily harm, the other for manslaughter. But compared with the Rhino-Princess combo, he was considered a mild-mannered gentleman.

None of the girls were paid for working the club. They rented "stage time" from the management, split their nightly take, and got to keep all their "tips." The cover charge and the insanely priced champagne and cigars kept management deeply in the black, to say nothing of its piece of any "special services" the girls chose to provide in the VIP Room.

As in all upscale strip clubs, the booze and cigars were a major source of untaxed revenue. The bartender was a short, thick-set Mexican, improbably known as "Gringo." An ex-boxer, he was still quick with his hands. He was quicker still with the .357 Magnum he kept under the bar, as two would-be holdup men had discovered the year before. The club's basement didn't just store stock, it doubled as a body-disposal system.

Everybody knew the deal: You get to the Double-X any way you can, and at your own risk. But once inside its parking area, you were as safe as in church. Safer, if the stories about the local archdiocese were to be believed.

♣

BUDDHA FOUND Cross at his private table that had been built into a triangulated corner of the joint. The unremarkable-looking man was watching a naked redhead table-dance for three guys in business suits, his face as expressionless as usual.

"What's happening, boss?"

"No incoming, either direction," Cross replied. "No business, no hostiles."

"Rhino says Princess hasn't been around. He's worried out of his mind about that looney-tune—wanted to speak to you. He's on duty, so I volunteered. Uh . . . you seen him around anywhere?"

"No," Cross said, stubbing out a cigarette in a black glass ashtray. The smoky light in the bar was just bright enough to illuminate the bull's-eye tattoo on the back of his hand.

"Yeah. Well, that guy's a stone head-case anyway. I mean, I don't see why you—"

"That's enough, Buddha. Princess is one of us. And that means"—Cross paused to look directly at the pudgy man—"he brought some baggage with him when he signed on. But he's stand-up to the max. Everybody in this crew has a reason to be here, right? The same reason."

"Right," Buddha admitted, as *Do you hate them? Do you hate them all?* flashed across the screen of his mind. "But he's been with us for years and we still don't know his MOS?"

"That, I haven't figured yet," the man called Cross acknowledged. He lit another cigarette, took a deep drag, and placed it in the ashtray. "There's a new girl working— she goes on soon. I'll be back to the joint in an hour or so."

♣

SIX HOURS later. An elderly man was semi-reclining behind the battered steel counter standing at the basement entrance to the Red 71 poolroom. He was watching a small black-and-white TV from under a green eyeshade.

A tall, handsome Latino entered, dressed in a full-drape

pink mohair jacket over a silky black shirt. He tapped on the counter with the underside of a heavy gold ring. After a long minute, the elderly man swiveled around to have a look.

"What?" he said, his voice a model of neutrality.

"I got a message for Cross," the Latino replied.

"Who?" the elderly man asked, a puzzled look on his face.

"Cross. You know. *El jefe*."

"I don't speak no Italian."

"Hey, old man, I don't have time for your little jokes— you just give this to him," the Latino said, sliding a folded square of white paper across the counter.

The elderly man made no move to pick it up. He read-justed his eyeshade and turned his attention back to the TV. The Latino waited and waited, but the elderly man never moved. Angrily, the Latino spun on his heel and walked out.

♣

CROSS UNFOLDED the square of white paper in the back room. He looked at the writing for a minute, shaking his head.

"Buddha, take a look at this."

The handwritten note was on heavy, watermarked paper. The script was flowery, ostentatiously serifed, obviously written with a calligraphic fountain pen.

We have el maricón. We know he is one of yours. We also know he did not join your team; he was taken. We know where you stole him from. We tell you this so that you under-stand. We know everything, from the beginning.

El maricón is now our property. If you wish to purchase him for a fair price, you must call 29-504-456-5588 tonight before midnight.

If you do not call, the next delivery will be a piece of our property, the work of our macheteros.

"They got Princess," Cross said, his voice barely audible.

"It don't sound like they know what they're doing, who-ever they are," Buddha reflected. "I mean, Princess plays the role and all, but that's just to get into fights—he's about as gay as a damn tomcat on Viagra."

"If it's the people I think it was, they do. I saw the light was on," Cross said, nodding his head in the direction of a red bulb hanging from an exposed wire. "So Rhino took off. Maybe he'll be able to tell us something when he comes back."

"What do you think they want, boss?"

"Money or blood," Cross answered, closing his eyes. "There's nothing else people like them *could* want."

♣

"**HE JUST** rode around," Rhino reported an hour later. "Fancy car. Red Ferrari—I couldn't have lost him if I tried. But all he did was drive. Finally, he pulled into an underground garage, a high-rise on the lakefront. No way to tell if he lives there—the garage was open to the public, too."

"How come you came back?"

"Tracker's on him now. I reached out on the cellular while I was still rolling. You were right to pull him away from those government guys. Tracker, he's one of us, no question."

"The guy in the Ferrari had a cell, too," Cross said. "See this note? The number they want me to call, that's a sat phone. Looks like it started in Honduras, but it could be bounced from anywhere by now."

"I didn't know—"

"Don't worry about it. It's SOP, follow anyone who comes

in here asking for me, right? You were already gone by the time I even saw the note. Maybe Tracker will come up with something."

"I find that fancy-boy, he'll tell us where Princess is," the giant muttered.

"If the guy who wrote the note was who I think he was, this guy in the Ferrari, he was just an errand boy."

"Who do you think was behind this? Who'd want to snatch *Princess*?" Rhino said, genuinely puzzled.

"It smells like Muñoz," Cross answered, lighting a cigarette. "And Muñoz always smells bad."

♣

TEN O'CLOCK that same night. Cross and Rhino stepped out on the darkened roof of the Red 71 building. They did a rapid circuit of the roof, ignoring the large wooden box with its several round openings. Satisfied, Cross took a heavy-looking hand phone from his pocket, punched in a number.

"Yes?" A voice in Latin-flavored English.

"Calling before midnight," Cross said.

"We have a package. And we think, maybe you like to trade us something for it?"

"I'm listening."

"A job. That's all. One job. You do it, you get your package back."

"Still listening."

"Not on this phone—you know better. Land line."

"Say it."

"There is a phone booth. Just off Lake Shore. You know where Michigan Avenue takes that big curve? Across the Drive, on the other side, there's a phone booth. It has a big red circle painted on the side. Tomorrow morning, at first light. You be there—you'll hear from us then," the Spanish-accented voice said, breaking the connection on the last word.

Cross looked at Rhino. "It's Muñoz all right," he said. "We should have thrown that *basura* in for free the last time."

♣

IT WAS 4:45 a.m. The city-camo'ed, blotchy gray-and-black sedan known as the "Shark Car" throughout the Badlands swept along Michigan Avenue, Buddha at the wheel.

Cross spotted the open-air phone booth marked with the promised red circle. Standing a few feet away was a black man in his late teens, dressed in the latest gangsta chic—gleaming gold high-tops on his feet, an L.A. Dodgers cap on his head, the brim turned to the side. He was walking in tiny circles, constantly glancing down to consult a beeper in his hand. Two members of his posse lounged nearby, leaning against a black Escalade with bright-blue rims.

Cross exited the Shark Car and starting walking toward the phone booth.

"Yo! Don't even think about it," the gangsta-garbed man snarled. "That there is *my* phone. Go find yourself another one, whitey—I got business."

Cross turned as if to walk away, and pulled a black semi-auto pistol from his coat in the same motion. "Me, too," he said quietly, holding the pistol aimed at the man's stomach.

The leader glanced over at his crew, but their hands were already high in the air. Buddha stood across from them, the three forming an isosceles triangle. It wasn't the tiny Sig Sauer P238 in his hand which had riveted the other two men; it was the laser dot Buddha was languidly playing across their chests.

"No disrespect," Cross told the leader, almost eerily calm. "Like you said, it's your phone. I'm waiting on this *one* important call, okay? Soon as it's over, you get your phone back, permanent. And you never see us again. Okay?"

"Yeah, all right, man," the leader said, his eye on the pistol.

"Only thing, I need privacy for my call, understand?"

"Yeah. Yeah, man. Don't get crazy. We just jet, all right?"

"I'd appreciate that," Cross said.

The leader backed away toward the Escalade. He climbed into the back seat, keeping his hands in plain sight. The other two jumped into the front. The big SUV took off, scattering gravel.

Any thoughts its occupants might have of turning around vanished when each side mirror of their SUV popped its glass, as if a pebble had been thrown up from the gravel by the huge tires. A soundless pebble.

Cross stood next to the phone booth, again visually reconfirming the large red circle spray-painted on its side. He picked up the phone, tossed in three quarters, listened for a dial tone to verify the line worked, and quickly replaced the receiver.

He lit a cigarette, took a deep drag.

Traffic was still sporadic. The partygoers were all off the street, and the commuters still hadn't made their appearance. Cross took a third pull on his cigarette, then snapped it away.

The sky began to lighten. Cross and Buddha didn't speak, didn't move from their spots. Their pistols were no longer in sight. Only their eyes were active, working in the overlapping full-circle sweeps they had learned together many years before.

♣

A LUSTROUS gray-white pigeon swooped down and perched atop the phone booth. Cross eyeballed the bird closely. It was markedly different from the winged rats that so thoroughly populated the city. This one had the same characteristically small head, short neck, and plump body, but its bearing was almost regal. And it was groomed to the max, every feather in place.

Cross nodded to himself as he spotted the tiny cylinder anchored to one of the pigeon's legs. He approached cautiously, even though the pigeon showed no signs of spooking. Cross reached up and stroked the bird before pulling it gently against his chest. He opened the cylinder, extracted a small roll of paper. The pigeon fluttered its wings once, hopping back onto the phone booth.

Cross unfurled the paper, his eyes focusing in on the tiny, precise writing.

WE ARE PROFESSIONALS, LIKE YOU. A MEETING MUST BE MADE SAFE FOR US BOTH. WE WILL NOT COME TO YOUR PLACE, AND YOU DO NOT KNOW WHERE WE ARE. WE WILL MEET AT NOON TOMORROW ON STATE STREET, AT THE OUTDOOR BISTRO CALLED NOSTRUM'S. YOU KNOW WHERE IT IS, WE ARE SURE. IF YOU ARE COMING, YOU MUST COME ALONE. WRITE YOUR DECISION ON THIS PAPER. IT WILL BE RETURNED TO US.

Cross took a felt-tipped pen from his jacket, scrawled the single word "*sí*" on the bottom of the note, and replaced the paper inside the pigeon's courier pouch. The bird preened itself for a few seconds and then took off, climbing higher and higher into the morning sky with powerful thrusts of its wings.

♣

LATE THAT night, the crew was gathered in the basement of Red 71.

"You did the recon?" Cross asked Buddha.

"Yeah. And I don't like it, boss. The tables are all outside, pretty spread out. It's only set back maybe ten, fifteen feet from the sidewalk. All wrong for a drive-by: too much foot traffic, and half of those yuppies must have cell-phone cameras. Wrong neighborhood. Too upscale—cops'd be *all* over it in seconds. But, even with all that, if they wanted to give it a try, you'd never see it coming."

Cross turned to the giant standing against the wall, watching. "Rhino?"

"The rooftop across the street's even worse. Anyone could get up there easy enough. But there's more than one way to do that, and we couldn't cover every spot."

Cross drew a series of intersecting lines on the pad in front of him, eyes down. He took two final drags from his cigarette before he stubbed it out.

"What it comes down to is, who's gonna make the meet for their side? If it's Muñoz himself, he's got to know we can blow him away if he tries anything. Even if he nailed me, he'd be a dead man a few seconds later. But if it's some flunky, Muñoz wouldn't give a rat's ass what happens to him. For all we know, Muñoz could be over the border, giving his orders from there."

"So . . . ?" Buddha queried.

"So this. Rhino, *you* take the roof across the street. Take it *early*. Anyone else shows up after you, just leave them there. We get Ace to work the sidewalk. They won't make him for our crew—he wasn't on the bust-out down in their territory. Buddha, you get us a cab from someplace, all right? Park it if you can find a spot, cruise it if you can't. Short loops, okay?"

"But what if they—?"

"Doesn't matter, so long as we move before they do. I'm

gonna roll up just at noon, like they said. If I spot Muñoz at the table, I go ahead and sit down. So, if you *don't* see me take a seat, that means it's me they want. Rhino already has the target locked on, so he takes out whoever's at the table in place of Muñoz.

"I'll handle anyone coming toward me. Ace will have my six. And Buddha can spray a lot of lead from the cab, if it turns out we need cover fire."

"And me?"

"You're on the roof, too," Cross told Tracker. "But on the roof of Nostrum's, so you'll be shooting straight down."

"You think it really could be like that, boss? Personal?" Buddha asks.

"Anyone else, I'd say no. But with Muñoz, it could be," Cross replied. "He talks professional, but he always was unstable."

♣

THE NEXT day, Cross emerged from the underground train station on State Street at 11:56 a.m., and headed east. It was already 11:59 when he first spotted Nostrum's, and a few seconds before noon when he saw a man he recognized, sitting at a table by himself. Cross kept his eyes only on that man as he approached, hands empty at his sides.

He sat down across from a copper-complected man who wore his thick hair pulled straight back, tied in a braided ponytail.

"Cross," the man said, not offering to shake hands. He wasn't engaging in any welcoming ceremony, merely stating a fact.

"Muñoz."

"Good afternoon, gentlemen," a voice interrupted their stare-down. "My name is Lance. I'll be serving you today.

Our house specials today are a baby-spinach salad with a mild vinaigrette dressing, together with—"

"That will be perfect," Muñoz said, his English laced with a regal touch of Castilian. "Bring us each one of those. But first . . . you have Ron Rico?"

"Yes, we do," the waiter replied. "But if I could perhaps suggest—"

"Bring me a double," Muñoz cut him off again. "And for my friend here . . ."

"Water," Cross said.

"We have San Pellegrino, and also a new—"

"Water," Cross repeated.

The waiter flounced off. "I hate them," Muñoz spat out.

"Who?"

"You know what I mean. *Los maricones.* You must know. After all, one of your own crew—"

"Princess. Yeah. He went along nice and easy?" Cross asked, his face still an unreadable blank.

"*Dios mío*, no!" Muñoz smiled, showing off a very expensive set of teeth. "That is one *hard* man, no matter that he is not really a man at all. First, he pulls out a pistol the size of a small house. The *noise* . . . like a cannon. It blew up one of our cars like a mortar strike!

"And *then* he killed two of my best men. With his bare hands! I held an Uzi on him, but he only laughed. If Lupe had not shot him, we would still be—"

"You shot him?" Cross asked, suddenly *very* soft-voiced.

"With a tranquilizer dart, *amigo*. Like you would use on a mad dog. It was loaded with enough juice to drop a gorilla. But even with the dart still in him, he continued to fight. I wonder how such a magnificent warrior—"

"What do you want?" Cross interrupted, no impatience in his voice.

"I already told you, *hombre*. I want you to do a job for us. Then you get your merchandise back."

"I don't read minds."

"You see this?" Muñoz asked, as he slid a tiny microchip across the marble tabletop.

Cross didn't touch the chip. "So?"

"So this is what we need," Muñoz answered. "Watch closely." He grasped the chip with the thumb and forefinger of each hand and pulled it apart, revealing one male and one female coupling. "We have this one," he said, holding up the male piece. "The other one, the mate, that is in the hands of another."

"Who?"

"Right to the point, yes? *Justo lo suficiente*. You know Humberto Gonzales? He works out of a bunch of connected apartments on the West Side."

Cross shook his head.

"No matter. We will tell you where he is, and you will take our property from him."

"How can you be sure—?"

"It is always with him, Cross. Always on his person. There was no one he could trust with it. But we have very good sources inside his organization. We know *exactly* where to look. It is in his right arm."

"*In* his arm?"

"On his right arm, right here," Muñoz said, patting his right biceps to illustrate. "He has a big tattoo. Of a dancing girl. Very pretty. The chip is somewhere under that tattoo. Implanted. A fine piece of surgery. So. We need his arm. You bring it to us, your job is done. That very instant, we return your . . . friend."

"No."

"What do you mean, no? Why do you say this?"

"What am I supposed to do, Muñoz? Pack the arm in dry ice and send it FedEx? You wouldn't give me a delivery address. And I'm sure not meeting you to hand it over in person.

"So here's how it's gonna happen," Cross continued. "Send that pigeon of yours—the chip would fit in his carry-pouch easy enough if it's the same size as that one there," Cross finished, pointing at the microchip lying on the tabletop.

"*Bueno!* That is a good plan, *hombre*. As soon as our bird is home, we will release your man . . . or whatever he is."

"What's on the chip?"

"That is not your business, my friend."

"Then get somebody else to do it."

"I do not think you understand. . . ."

"I understand just fine. I don't think *you* do. Things have changed around here since nine/eleven. There's jobs I don't take. Now, what's on the chip?"

Muñoz stroked his chin. Cross lit a cigarette and took a deep drag. A long minute passed, during which Cross took two more drags and stubbed out his cigarette.

The waiter approached with a pair of glasses on a tray. "Here you are, gentlemen. Your salads will be along in a few minutes."

Muñoz waved him away, leaning forward so his eyes were locked on Cross. "You speak *español*, yes?"

"*Poquito.*"

"You know the word *favela?*"

"No."

"It is Portuguese. A language half shared. It means 'slum,' but not as you Americans speak of such places. I was born in a *favela*. In the hills just outside of Rio, built on land used to bury toxic waste, right next to a huge dump site for garbage. A mountain of people, one tiny shack of tin and wood on top of another. Just to get water would take a whole day."

"Why tell me?"

"A *favela* makes your prisons look like palaces. There are three ways out. I do not play football—what you call 'soccer' —and I cannot sing."

"So you went into dope. *That's* what you think I need to know?"

"No, *hombre*. What you need to know is only this: I would kill a thousand times—a thousand *cities*—rather than return to the *favela*."

"There's no reason to kill a man more than once."

"Ah, you joke when I try to . . . explain myself. *Muy bien*. So now *you* listen: Herrera had a couple of dozen locations. Locations where he stashed money. Money and product. He and I were partners. I have half of the microchip, but mine only works if snapped into his half. Same for him, of course.

"Now, Herrera, he was having a problem. I *know* he himself hired you to retrieve a certain book. But, after that, I hear nothing. Then I learn Herrera was killed. His car, his bodyguards . . . everything blown to pieces. So I know even more now. I know you were paid. Paid twice.

"Why do I say 'twice'? Because it is Humberto who has the chip, not Esteban. Why? Because we knew all along that Esteban was secret partners with Herrera. We speak of honor, but *betrayal*—that is the life we live. Partnerships mean nothing to a savage like Herrera. That old man, he was ready to eliminate Esteban, so perhaps Esteban also paid you to eliminate Herrera? That would be your style, would it not?"

Seeing Cross was not going to respond, or even change expression, Muñoz continued:

"My partnership with Humberto is no different than the one Herrera had with me, or Esteban with *him*. That is why we use the chips, so that each of us has nothing without the other. But our negotiations with Humberto have proved fruitless—he is greedy beyond tolerance. I want to go back across the border, and I want to *stay* there. But, first, I need Humberto's arm."

"What's my piece?" Cross said, his voice as expressionless as his face.

"Your piece? Your piece? I told you . . . you get *el maricón* returned to you."

"You got a good sense of humor, Muñoz. You want me to do all kinds of risky stuff to score something worth tens of millions to you, and you want to trade a POW in exchange? Do the math."

"This . . . Princess. He was your man. We have—"

"What you have is a soldier. A soldier who knew the deal when he signed on. I wouldn't want to lose him, but I could live with that a lot better than if there's anything on that microchip that would ring the wrong alarm bells. Those Homeland Security boys all carry open paper—they fill it in *after* they do whatever they want to.

"Don't get me wrong. In *our* country, nobody gives a damn about flags or uniforms. When we fight, we fight for only two reasons: self-defense or money. So I'll make it simple. Half a million. Cash. *And* Princess. For that, you get your little chip."

"You will trust me to—"

"You should take that act onstage, Muñoz. Sure, I'll trust you to release Princess. It wouldn't do you any good to dust him. You wouldn't make a dime, and you might get some of the wrong people angry at you if you did. People who can travel south anytime they want.

"But the cash . . . no way. You send a man. *Your* man, okay? We hand him the chip. He puts it in the pigeon's bag, and hands over the cash. The bird takes off. It lands wherever you taught it to. When it touches down, you try the chip. You see that it works, and then we're done. We hold on to your man until we see Princess, then your guy walks away. Got it?"

"What is to prevent you from killing my man and keeping the money? *And* the chip?"

"Don't play stupid. Half of that chip's no more use to me than it was to you. What I want is the money. And I want you back over the border, too. This job's gonna draw enough heat as it is."

"Your salads, gentlemen," the waiter interrupted again, placing a plate in front of each man. "Will there be anything—?"

"No," Muñoz snapped, eyes still on his opponent. Finally, he slid a folded piece of paper over to Cross. "It is all there. Everything you need. *Muy pronto*, eh?"

Cross lit another cigarette, ignoring his salad as he pocketed the paper. Then he leaned forward slightly, dropping his voice a notch. "You're a professional. So am I. We understand how these things are done. Money is money. Business is business. I'm gonna get you your little chip, Muñoz. You're gonna pay me my money and let my man go, are we clear?"

Muñoz nodded, warily.

"You know how soldiers are," Cross said, just above a whisper. "In war, you don't look too deep. A guy's good with explosives, another's a top sniper, maybe another's a master trail-reader. It all comes down to what you need. Turns out one of the guys you recruit is a little bent, you don't pay much attention to what he does when he's not in the field, you understand what I'm saying?"

Muñoz tilted his head slightly forward, waiting.

"Some people, they're in because they like it. It's not for the money—it's certain . . . opportunities they want. I got nobody like that in my crew. But maybe, just maybe, you do. Guys who might do something unprofessional, just because they *like* doing it. You can always spot them: the first ones who volunteer to do interrogations. Rapists. Torture freaks. You always got them sniffing around, looking for work, right?"

"So?" Muñoz challenged. "What has this to do with what I—?"

"You got my man, got him locked up. He's your hostage. I understand that. I don't expect you're gonna feed him whiskey and steak, send up a friend if he gets lonely. That's okay. But maybe you got guys on your team who like to hurt people. Hurt them for fun. That's not professional."

"Yes," Muñoz said impatiently. "I know all this."

"Herrera, he liked to watch men die. That's why he had those cage fights."

"Herrera is no more, *amigo*. You above all should know that."

"There's others like him. Maybe you have some of them in your crew. What I want to tell you is this: I can find one myself, easy enough."

"Why do you say all this? What is your meaning?" Muñoz spoke softly, but a titanium thread of menace throbbed in his voice.

"Just play it for real," Cross told him. "Nobody gets paid for acting stupid. You know about me. You know people who owe me. *Some* of them, anyway. You know what I can do.

"So listen good. If you hurt Princess, if we don't get him back in the same condition as you found him, we'll find *you*. Wherever you go, no matter how long it takes, we *will* find you, Muñoz. And when we do, it's going to take you a long time to die."

♣

"**HOW MUCH** do I owe you?" Rhino asked the waiter from Nostrum's. They were standing near the mouth of an alley that opened into a street in the heart of the gay cruising area.

"You owe me some respect," the waiter snapped. "I don't forget what Princess did for us. I'm a man," he said with quiet force. "A man pays his debts."

"I apologize," Rhino squeaked. "If there's ever—"

But the waiter was already walking away.

♣

IN THE basement of Red 71, Cross was using a laser pointer to illuminate various parts of a crudely drawn street map he had taped to the back wall.

"He's somewhere in here," Cross said, the thin red line of the laser pointer aimed at a cross section of a tall building standing next to three others exactly similar. "We don't know what apartment. We don't even know what floor. Humberto controls the buildings, so he may even switch from time to time."

"This Humberto, he never goes out?" Rhino asked.

"Once a week. To the airport. He meets an international flight on the south concourse. A different guy comes each time. Humberto meets this guy, talks to him for an hour or so; then the guy just turns around and gets back on another plane."

"The courier still has to clear customs," Buddha said. "Otherwise, what's the point?"

"Sure. It's a sterile corridor up to that point. No way to get in or out without the machines looking you over. But whoever comes in, he's not bringing product, he's bringing in a chip that's smaller than a wristwatch battery. Nobody would give it a second look. And even if they did, so what? It's a piece of plastic, not contraband. The courier clears customs, has a conversation with Humberto, and goes back home. That's all there is to it."

"Don't make sense," Buddha said. "That's a lot of gelt just to get around a wiretap."

"I don't think that's what it is," Cross said. "Like I said, I think the courier's bringing half of a puzzle. Like this one—" holding up the chip he got from Muñoz. "But the only way to see if it works is to try it: they all look alike. The way I got it figured, Herrera was playing both sides. Trying to get Humberto and Esteban to waste each other, each of them thinking they were partners with *him*, see?"

"So?" Buddha put in impatiently.

"So Herrera's not around anymore. But he probably had chips stashed all over the damn place. Maybe Humberto thinks Muñoz hasn't got the *only* one. Or maybe not even the right one. But it's still his best chance. They go through this negotiation dance, but it's really a stall for time."

"This Humberto, he cuts the chip out of his own arm every week?" Buddha said, skepticism heavy in his voice.

"Maybe not. Maybe he's got a dupe. I don't know. But this much isn't open for discussion: we've got to take Humberto at the airport. That job pays half a mil—that's a buck and a quarter apiece."

"You want to dust him at the airport, then chop off his arm right there? And—what?—throw it in an ice chest?" Ace asked caustically.

"No. We've got to bring him out of there, alive and in one piece. I think I know how to do it. Something I've been working on for a while.

"But Humberto won't come alone. So I figure we take him when he comes back out of the terminal. Just before he gets into his car. Buddha can get an ambulance real close. What we need is a hideout. Someplace close to the airport. Quiet enough for us to do the rest of the job."

"How you figure a hundred and a quarter apiece?" Rhino asked, leaning forward, his bulk imposing itself on the room.

"Me, you, Ace, and Buddha," Cross replied, puzzled. "Tracker won't take a dime, says he wants to prove in, first."

"Righteous," Ace said, touching the brim of his Zorro hat in a salute to a man not present.

"The way I figure it, Princess is in for a share, too," Rhino squeaked.

"Princess?! He's the genius who got us into this mess," Buddha spit out.

"Then he's the one who *brought* us the job," Rhino snapped back.

"So give him half *your* share," Buddha suggested.

Rhino slowly turned, focusing his small eyes on the short, pudgy man, not saying a word. Buddha gazed back, unfazed.

"Half a mil splits five ways real easy," Ace said.

Cross nodded.

Buddha waited for a slow count of ten, during which Rhino never blinked. "Yeah, fine. But if one of you ever mentions this to my wife—"

♣

CROSS PLUCKED the cell phone from his jacket pocket in response to a soft, insistent purr.

"Go!"

"He's in. On schedule," Buddha's voice was that of a man accustomed to speaking from cover, quiet but clear.

"You have his ride?"

"Black Mercedes. Four-door S-Class. Bodyguard left on foot so he could meet up when the target walks out. Driver's already out of the picture—replacement set."

"Roger that. So it's down to two . . . unless you scoped any backups?"

"Negative. Came in with driver and bodyguard, front seat; just him in the back."

"Then get rolling," Cross said, breaking the connection. He turned to Rhino. "They'll probably page the driver as they get close to the back exit. That way, he can pull out of the parking area, swing around, and be waiting when they step off the curb.

"He'll have another bodyguard hanging around, somewhere else. You take him. I'll get Humberto. Ace'll already be behind the wheel of their Mercedes, but they'll never get close enough to see that. You and me, we ride crash-car on the getaway; we all meet back at the spot if we get separated."

Rhino nodded. "You really think that contraption's gonna work?" he asked, pointing his index finger—the one with the missing tip—at what looked like a particularly awkward pistol: instead of a butt, the pistol's handle was a long, narrow canister.

"It's gas-propelled," Cross explained. "Same stuff they use in air conditioners. We should get around eleven hundred feet per second. And it won't make a sound."

"It only works for one shot?"

"One's all we get."

"Why don't we just finish this guy? What do we need him alive for?"

"Muñoz wants him dead," Cross said. "But he's only paying us for an arm, not a body."

♣

THE PHONE purred again. Cross snapped it to his ear. "What?"

"Moving." Buddha's voice. "Me, too. You got two minutes, tops."

"Moving," Cross echoed, pointing a finger at the windshield. Rhino keyed the motor of the Shark Car, threw it into gear. Cross was punching a number into his phone.

Twenty seconds later, he said "Go!" and closed his phone.

♣

HUMBERTO WAS standing on the wide curb, a broad-chested man at his side, obviously that on-scene bodyguard Cross had been expecting. The bodyguard spotted the Mercedes rolling toward them and stepped forward, reaching for the handle to the back door.

Cross moved out of the shadows cast by a thick concrete pillar, the gas gun up and aimed. Humberto grabbed at his neck as he fell. His bodyguard whirled just in time to meet a .22 hollow-point with his left eye.

Rhino pocketed his silenced pistol and charged forward, carrying Humberto's body in one hand as another might a suitcase. The Mercedes pulled off.

An ambulance rolled in, its rear doors popping open. Rhino tossed Humberto inside. The ambulance doors closed as it took off for the exit, lights flashing. Rhino ran to the Shark Car and jumped into the open back door, his movements acrobatic despite his bulk. Cross, now behind the wheel, mashed the pedal. The Shark Car chased the ambulance, easily passing it within a half-mile.

When the Airport Police arrived, they found one dead man, devoid of identification. And no shortage of highly contradictory accounts from spectators.

♣

THE AMBULANCE pulled to a stop in the shadows of a bridge abutment, just a few yards off the freeway. The Shark Car was already waiting—Cross had placed the anonymous vehicle so that it would be parallel to the ambulance.

He stood watch as Rhino threw Humberto's limp body over his shoulder and transferred it to the Shark Car's trunk.

Buddha took the wheel of the Shark Car; Cross moved to the shotgun seat. Ace and Rhino took the back, weapons out, each man covering a different rear window.

As the Shark Car pulled away, Buddha said: "I spray-dusted as good as I could, boss. But you never know what they're gonna find when they vacuum that bus."

Cross pulled a small radio transmitter from his jacket, checked the blinking red LED, and tripped a toggle switch. A heavy, thumping *whoosh!* followed. The sky behind them became a red-and-yellow fireball.

"What they're gonna find is some dead meat," Cross told Buddha. "Well done."

♣

AS THE Shark Car entered a quiet community of tract houses, the phone in Cross's jacket sounded. He opened it up, but didn't speak.

"Clear at six." Tracker's voice.

Cross broke the connection and gave the thumbs-up signal to the men in the back seat.

♣

BUDDHA PULLED into a driveway of packed dirt, nosing the car forward until it was inside a garage whose doors had swung open in response to an electronic signal.

He popped the trunk. Rhino reached in and grabbed Humberto's still-limp form by his belt.

Five minutes later, Humberto was strapped to a straight chair in the basement of the house. The men waited another half-hour. Despite Tracker's assurance, each stayed watchful and alert against the possibility they had been followed.

Finally, Cross stood up and slipped a stocking mask over his face. "All clear," he said quietly. "Let's get to it."

♣

"**THAT SHOULD** be enough," Rhino said, as he squeezed the plunger of a hypodermic, testing it for clearance. He compressed Humberto's arm with one huge hand, tapped a prominent vein, and drove the needle home with a surgeon's precision.

Cross waited as the adrenaline mix slowly took hold, watched as Humberto gradually regained consciousness. He signaled Rhino to stay where he was—looming over Humberto's back, but not visible.

"Wha . . . What is this?" Humberto mumbled, his eyes struggling for focus.

"It's a job, pal," Cross said. "You do what you're told, it *stays* a job. You don't . . ." He let his voice trail off, its message clear.

"You're not . . ." Humberto said, his vision gradually clearing.

"What we are is professionals," Cross replied. "Just like you. We get paid for our work. Just like you."

"What work?"

"Muñoz paid us. For your arm."

Humberto went deathly white under his swarthy skin. "I don't know what—"

"Yeah, you do," Cross interrupted. "You got something Muñoz wants. A microchip. Someplace in your right arm. Muñoz, he paid us to bring him that arm."

"Wait! *Wait* a minute! I can—"

"Don't say anything. Listen to our offer. Then you say yes or you say no. That's all the choices you get. Understand?"

Humberto nodded, his hooded eyes now steadied on Cross.

"We *are* gonna get that microchip. We know it's somewhere under that tattoo. We can take it gentle," Cross said, "or we can take it hard. Your choice."

"I *have* no choice," Humberto said, his voice calming as strength flowed back into him.

"Muñoz, he has one of my men. He wants to trade him for that chip," Cross told Humberto. "But if we saw off your whole arm like he wants, he gets *you*, too. And he didn't pay us for a kill . . . just for the chip."

"*I* could pay you . . ." Humberto said.

"That's right, you could. But then what would you have? Your bodyguard's gone. So is your driver. And Muñoz would *still* know where that chip was. You know how he must have found out—you've got a traitor close to you, and you don't know who that is. Might take Muñoz longer the next time, but you'd end up just as dead."

"What do you suggest?" Humberto asked, a faint ray of hope sounding in his voice.

"I *suggest* you pay us. Not to leave your arm alone—to take out Muñoz. The chip, that's what gets us in the door, see? And once we get in there, we sit down with Muñoz. Only he never gets up. Costs you a flat two million. Cash."

"I can get—"

"No," Cross cut him off. "Forget the games. You're not making any phone calls. Not writing any notes, either. You're too smart not to have some money stashed. Serious money. And you'd never trust anyone with *that* info. I'm betting you got it nice and accessible. No safe-deposit boxes, no passwords . . . nothing like that."

Cross put a cigarette into the thin slit cut into his mask and lit it with the same hand.

"So it goes like this: you tell us where the money is. Tell us right now. One of my crew goes there, picks it up. If it's in more than one place, that's okay—just takes us a little longer. When my man comes back here with the cash, we count out two mil for ourselves, give you the rest, if there is any. And *then* we do the job for you."

"How do I know you won't just take the money—take *all* the money—and kill me anyway?"

"If I was gonna do that, what would I need this mask for?" Cross said, deliberately calling attention to the makeshift balaclava covering his face and neck. "This is business, that's all. You didn't come after us. It wasn't you who snatched my man and held him for ransom. That's all on Muñoz. So it's Muñoz who has to go. I'm just making sure we get paid for our work, see?"

"And if I say no?"

"Didn't I say that Muñoz snatched one of my men? So Muñoz, he's *already* dead. But we have to get close enough to kill him. If we can't use the chip to get us in the door, we'll just bring him your arm."

A long minute passed. Humberto took a deep breath. "It's right under her butt," he said, flexing his right biceps, which sent the tattooed dancer into a very realistic bump-and-grind. "Have you got a drink for a man first?"

♣

HUMBERTO WAS in a comfortable easy chair, his feet up on an ottoman. He was bare-chested, a gauze bandage taped around his right biceps. To his left, a water glass half full of dark liquid sat on an end table. A thick cigar smoldered in an ashtray. Humberto's handsome face was relaxed.

"Listen to me, *amigo*," he said to Cross. "The key to Muñoz is his pride. Muñoz was always . . . *muy macho, comprende?* Years ago, he fought a duel. With machetes. It was a matter of honor. He is very, very good with blades. And with his hands, even better—very quick, very strong."

"And you tell me this because . . . ?"

"Because now I trust you, *hombre*. And I want to prove it to you."

"You think that does it? Telling me about this guy's ego?"

"No," Humberto said, his dark eyes steady on the black stocking mask covering Cross's head. "*This* is what does it: I know who you are."

"Is that right?"

"Yes. You are the man they call Cross. You hide your face, but you forget to cover your hands," Humberto said, flicking his glance at the back of Cross's right hand, where a bull's-eye tattoo stood out in bold relief. "I myself hired you once before. Years ago. I know your markings."

Cross made a sound of disgust, reached up, and pulled off the stocking mask. "Tell me what you know."

"I know you—your crew—you were the ones who killed Herrera. I was not there, but I have heard about it, from many places. Some believed you wanted his product, but I know you don't play in my game—I always believed you took his stash of jewels instead. I know Esteban always converted his product to money. Only gold, diamonds, the *true* hard currency."

"What else?"

"Esteban became too strong for his own good. And Herrera, *he* was a devil. *El diablo* does not take in partners." Humberto's shoulders moved in an eloquent shrug. "As for Muñoz, I know there was a battle, years ago. Many died. But you escaped. That was all I know. That and the tattoo on your hand. It must have been some kind of rescue operation, which was why Muñoz was not killed.

"Still, Muñoz always swore he would pay you back—he lost much prestige when you invaded his compound. He had to return all the protection money Herrera had paid him.

That hurt him as well. When you got away that time, you took some piece of Muñoz with you.

"I heard more things, later. Herrera, he hired you to do something. Something involving Esteban. And now both men are dead."

"Why tell me all this?" Cross asked.

"Because I paid for Esteban. Me. It was all my money, even if Herrera acted as if he was the one in charge. Esteban, he was a good front, but he was nothing but an actor, playing a role. We never met face to face, but I know it was you I paid—Herrera would not have known who to call upon, but I did. Like I said, from before.

"You did your work well, Cross. Herrera is gone. Soon, Muñoz will be, too. But you cannot run a drug network yourself. You do not have the contacts down south. You and me, both professionals, I think maybe we will be partners."

"Like you said, not my game," Cross answered.

♣

"**IT'S DONE**," Cross said into the mouthpiece of the cell phone.

"Yes, I watch the news on television," came the voice of Muñoz. "But it is *not* done. Only half."

"I'm ready to finish it. Now."

"You know the King Hotel? On Wabash, near—"

"I know it."

"My man will be standing in front, on the sidewalk, at midnight. You take him wherever you want. Once you are satisfied that we have not followed you, send us the chip."

"How are we gonna get the pigeon?"

"*Pigeon!* You insult me. My man will have the bird with him. In a cage."

"And my money?"

"*Sí, compañero.*"

♣

"**THE KING** Hotel ain't nothing," Ace said, facing the assembled crew. "I got a half-dozen people in that dump. It's a low-class dive. A little dice game downstairs, but mostly it's nothing but a hot-sheet. I can be inside hours before they show, cover you anywhere from the top floor down."

"Perfect," Cross said. "Buddha, you make the pickup, all right? Me and Rhino, we'll transport Humberto's man. Now everybody get to work wiping things down—we can't have another fire so soon."

♣

FROM INSIDE the front door of the King Hotel, all the watchful desk clerk could see was the back of a medium-height man in a blue jacket. The man looked as if he was waiting for a bus, smoking a cigarette. Only two discordant notes sounded. At the man's feet was a large cage, draped in black with a brass-ring handle at the top. And a bright-red dot of light holding steady right between the man's shoulder blades. The red dot tracked the man, moving as he moved.

The Shark Car pulled to the curb. The back door opened. Some words were exchanged. The waiting man climbed into the car, pulling the cage behind him. The car took off.

A few minutes later, the desk clerk saw a slim, fine-featured black man coming down the stairs, a cut-down, double-barreled shotgun in one hand. The desk clerk purposefully did not meet the man's eyes. When he looked up, the man was gone, almost as if he had never been there.

The desk clerk didn't react. But it wasn't the two hundred dollars sitting atop the desk that earned his silence. The clerk knew what the red dot on the waiting man's back had meant, and he didn't want one on his own. Ever.

♣

THE SHARK Car worked its way through the Badlands, heading for Red 71 as unerringly as the homing pigeon it carried in its back seat. The phone on the seat next to Buddha chirped. The pudgy man picked it up and flicked a switch with his thumb. "Go," he said.

"All clear here." Cross's voice.

"Coming in," Buddha replied. "ETA ten minus."

"Roger that. Six still clear?"

"The full one eighty."

Buddha clicked off the phone, his eyes flicking back and forth between the road and the rearview mirror. He pulled the Shark Car through a fresh gap in the chain-link fence, and parked just behind the back door to Red 71.

He slapped the back door three times with the flat of his hand. It opened immediately. Cross stepped to one side, covering the area with a stubby machine pistol. Buddha entered first. Then the man they had picked up. Rhino was the last to go inside, blocking the only way out with both his bulk and the ridiculous gold Desert Eagle .50-caliber semi-auto that Princess had purchased years ago . . . because it was so pretty.

In the basement, Rhino hand-searched the courier, his touch delicate and sensitive. When he nodded an okay, Cross came forward and ran an electronic wand over the courier's body. "Relax," he said to the man. "Have a seat."

The man seated himself in an overstuffed chair, reached into his pocket to light a cigarette.

"What do they call you?" Cross asked.

"I am Lopez."

"Okay, Lopez. *Dónde está el dinero?*"

Lopez's lips twisted into a thin smile that did not show his teeth. "In the cage, *hombre*. In the bottom of the cage. If you will permit me . . ."

Cross nodded, and the man got to his feet. He walked over to the cage and gently flicked the black cover off. Inside was the big-chested pigeon Cross had seen before.

"This is *el bailador del cielo*," Lopez said, stroking the pigeon's chest, "the dancer of the sky." He reached inside and removed the bird, cradling it softly. "Pick up the floor of the cage," he said to Cross.

Cross studied the cage for a long minute, then removed the newspaper from the cage floor, revealing a flat metal plate with a ring in the center. He pulled the ring and the floor came off.

"What the hell does Muñoz think I'm gonna do with gold bars?" he said to Lopez. "All this has to be washed—I can't just go out and spend it."

"Money . . . bills would not fit in such a small space, *hombre*," Lopez replied. "Señor Muñoz said you would have . . . resources. And that you could assay the gold yourself, as well."

Cross nodded, his fingers stroking the strange blue scar on his cheekbone, wondering why it burned at times. Rhino scooped up the gold bars into one giant hand.

"Okay, how do you want to do this?" Cross asked.

"First, I check the chip. With this . . ." Lopez said, taking a mate from his shirt pocket. "You could never duplicate the chip, and certainly not so quickly. If it plugs into the one I have, we will know you have completed your part of the bargain."

"Do it," Cross said; he took the chip from his jacket and handed it over.

Lopez carefully aligned the two chips. They came together with an audible snapping sound. "*Bueno!* This the one."

"And now . . . ?" Cross asked.

"Now you put the chip right here," Lopez said, tapping the tiny cylinder on the bird's right claw, just above the talon. "Then he flies home. Straight home. You will see—if you care to check—that you cannot fit a transmitter into his pouch. And if you attach one anywhere else, *el bailador* will not fly. You understand?"

"Yeah," Cross said, still stroking the tiny blue scar. *It's more like a brand,* he thought to himself, not for the first time. After a few moments, he abruptly left the room.

♣

"**WE'RE READY** to go," Cross said into the cell phone.

"When will you—?"

"I gotta talk to him first."

"Talk to who?"

"My man. The one you got."

"I told you—"

"I don't care what you *told* me," Cross said. "We're in the end-game now. You want to talk to *your* man, I can do that. You want to play games, you're going to force us to do the same."

"Call back in thirty minutes," Muñoz said. "And have Lopez with you."

♣

"**YOU WANT** to speak to your man?" Cross spoke into the phone.

"*Sí.* Put him on."

"Yes, I am here, *jefe*," Lopez said, calmly. "Everything was as it should be." He said "*Sí, sí,*" rapidly and handed the phone to Cross.

"Your turn," Cross said into the mouthpiece.

"*Momentito.*"

Another minute passed; then Cross heard the unmistakable voice of Princess. "I'm good," the armor-muscled man-child said. "These little punks got me trussed up like a turkey, but they haven't done nothing to me."

"They feeding you?"

"Just garbage. I'm probably down to three fifteen with all the crap they serve here. They don't even have any of my special supplements. And—"

"Okay, Princess, just calm down, all right? They'll be cutting you loose soon."

"Are you satisfied?" Muñoz's voice cut in. "Are you ready to release our bird?"

"Tomorrow," Cross said. "Tomorrow at first light."

"Why not now, *hombre*? Our bird can fly at night."

"I need a few hours. There's some things I have to do to make sure you guys are playing it straight. First light. When Princess shows up, we'll let your man go."

"*Adios,*" Muñoz said, and hung up.

♣

"HE'S OKAY?" Rhino asked, anxiety making his voice even squeakier than usual.

"He said 'supplements,'" Cross replied. "You know what that means. He's all right, but he doesn't see a way out of there. If he'd said 'vitamins,' he'd have an exit spotted. If he didn't say *either* word, it would be a trap. So I don't think they messed with him."

"You think they'll actually let him go?" Buddha asked.

"Would *you*?" Cross answered.

♣

THE NEXT morning, dawn was slowly breaking through a blue-black night sky as Lopez stood on the roof of Red 71, the pigeon in his hands.

"Do it," Buddha told him.

"*Volar!*" Lopez commanded, tossing the pigeon into the air. The bird climbed, then banked, wings working smoothly.

A few seconds later, a tiny bird blasted out of Cross's leather-gloved hand, its blue-gray wings a blur in the sky, a distinctive *killy-killy-killy* trilling from its beak. The bird soared like an F-16, a blur in the vision of the watchers on the roof who were tracking the bird through binoculars. Cross picked up his phone.

"Airborne."

Cross closed his phone, said, "Let's go," to Buddha. As Buddha turned to follow Cross downstairs, Rhino's murderous hand curled around the back of Lopez's neck.

♣

"**I DON'T** get it, boss," Buddha said. "I know we got a transmitter on that mini-hawk of yours, but I've seen that thing in action—no way their pigeon's gonna make it back home."

"East," Cross said into his cell phone, watching a small round blue screen set into an electronic box he held between his legs. "Holding steady. You on it?"

"Total," Rhino's voice.

"It's not a hawk," Cross absently said to Buddha. "It's a kestrel. A falcon, okay? I got a mated pair up there. The female's sitting on some eggs. The male brings food. I haven't fed them for days—wouldn't let them loose to get food for themselves, either. They usually hit small birds, like sparrows. But I've got the male trained to hit pigeons—he really loves them."

"Yeah, but . . ."

"But what?"

"You got your bird all stoked up, I get that. But that's only gonna make him knock that pigeon right out of the sky. Then how in hell are we gonna—?"

"Kestrels only take prey near the ground," Cross explained. "Muñoz will wait until his pigeon touches down. By the time he gets close enough to look in its pouch, it's Kaddish for his little 'sky dancer.'"

Urban scenery flew past the windows of the Shark Car as Cross continued to give directions to Buddha in person and to Rhino over the phone.

"What's his name?" Buddha asked.

"Who?"

"The bird, Chief. The . . . kestrel or whatever you call it."

"Name?" Cross said, clearly puzzled. "It's a bird."

Buddha shrugged, and went back to work, handling the big car expertly, as always.

♣

"**HE'S HEADING** for the flats," Cross said into the phone. "No place else he *could* be going. You got visual?"

"Locked on," Rhino replied. "He's sitting right above the pigeon. Just hovering. Ready to dive."

"The *second* that pigeon starts his drop, we move," Cross said. "Stay tight."

♣

"**GOT 'EM,**" Rhino's voice squeaked. "It's a three-story. Clubhouse on the first floor. Says *Los Amigos* on the door. Right on the waterfront, at the end of Pine Street."

"You sure?"

"Dead sure. The pigeon's dropping down, heading for home. And your bird, he's still just . . . hovering."

"Cars in front?"

"Only one. A white . . . Lincoln, it looks like. I can see . . . Wait! I got it! There's a coop on the roof. Whole bunch of birds up there. It has to be—"

"*Go!*" Cross barked, breaking the connection.

The Shark Car's front tires lifted slightly off the ground from the sudden blast of acceleration as Buddha tapped the first nitrous switch. The target building came into view just as they spotted Rhino's recently stolen Montero heading toward the back.

"Here he comes!" Rhino squeaked as the kestrel went into a power dive. The pigeon may have seen the kestrel's shadow, or it may have been alerted by its primitive sensors. Its wings fluttered desperately, seeking the shelter of the coop.

Just before the pigeon touched down, the kestrel struck, its tiny talons balled into fists, stunning its prey. The pigeon staggered away, its damaged wing barring any escape.

Muñoz ran onto the roof. He sprinted toward the pigeon, waving his arms to scare off the intruder, but the kestrel calmly mounted its prey, tearing at the flesh of the pigeon's chest.

Muñoz slashed at the kestrel with a machete, but the tiny falcon danced away, its baleful unblinking eyes now trained on its new enemy.

Muñoz thrust his body between the pigeon and the kestrel, frantically clawing at the pigeon's courier pouch.

A series of explosions sounded below—flash-bang grenades thrown through the glass windows of the bar. Muñoz heard machine-gun fire. A thin smile played across his lips. With one mighty swipe of his machete, he chopped the pigeon in half, then scrambled on his hands and knees to recover the courier pouch. The kestrel watched calmly, continuing to tear apart the other half of the pigeon Muñoz left behind.

The rooftop now held a pair of predators, each absorbed in its own work, totally unconcerned with the other's.

Downstairs, Rhino swept the ground floor with a long blast from his M-4, screaming "Princess!" at the top of his lungs.

Two men charged down the stairs, and were immediately cut down by a blast from Ace's shotgun. Cross pointed at Buddha, who was working his way along the wall, his modified Sig out and ready.

At Buddha's nod, Cross pointed to an open door. As soon as Buddha started to move, Ace began to climb the stairs, chest flat against the wall, gun arm extended as a probe.

Buddha stepped carefully down the darkened stairway. Suddenly, he spotted Princess in a far corner, the bodybuilder's chest crossed with heavy chains like bandoliers.

Princess's head lolled against his chest—Buddha could see only the top of his shaven skull. He holstered his pistol, eyes sweeping the room for any sign of a key to unlock the chains.

A shot rang out, catching Buddha in the left shoulder. The pudgy man went down and rolled, whipping out his pistol and returning fire in the same smooth motion.

A muffled grunt of pain from the deep recesses of the basement told Buddha his shot had hit home. He changed direction, crawling until he was next to Princess. Then he popped straight up, firing a short, sweeping burst from his pistol at the same time.

With all his remaining strength, Buddha braced one foot against the chair Princess was strapped into and shoved, toppling the bodybuilder to the floor. More shots peppered the wall behind him.

Buddha scrambled so that his own body was covering

most of the fallen Princess, calmly ejecting the magazine from his pistol and snapping in another. Then he called out *¡Vamos!* as a challenge to anyone who wanted to come closer.

♣

MUÑOZ POCKETED the microchip and started down the stairs, a machete in one hand. On the third-floor landing, he cat-footed his way toward the rearmost room. He stepped inside, then satisfied himself that his escape rope was still anchored to the floor.

The drug lord had a car waiting below. If his luck held, he could be on his way to safety in seconds. As he gathered the rope to himself, Cross walked into the room, an Army-issue .45 in his hand.

Muñoz turned to face his sworn enemy. He stood with his legs spread apart, the machete now held in both his hands.

Cross held his weapon in both hands as well, aimed at the chest of the kidnapper.

For a few seconds, there was nothing but silence. Neither man noticed a thin black splotch at the edge of the room.

"So, *hombre*," Muñoz said. "It must always come to this, no?" Suddenly, he flung his machete point-first at the floor, where it stuck, quivering from the sheer force of its entry.

The black splotch quivered, too, as if in harmony with the machete.

The tiny blue brand on Cross's face began to burn.

Muñoz moved slowly toward Cross, hands curled into claws. "You always wanted to know, didn't you, Cross? *¿Quién es más hombre?* Any coward can fight with weapons. A real man fights with nothing more than his own hands.

"Now we see, yes?" Muñoz snarled, as his entire body flowed into a hand-combat crouch.

"No," Cross answered, pulling the trigger of his .45. The

heavy slug took Muñoz in the stomach, knocking him to his knees.

Standing over Muñoz, who was writhing on the floor in horrific pain but still clawing with his hands, Cross carefully emptied the magazine of his .45 into the dying man's skull. Cross released the magazine of his pistol, slammed in a fresh one, and turned to the door. He never noticed the ace of spades and the jack of clubs floating toward the ceiling. Nor the still-burning blue scar on his cheek.

♣

IN THE basement of Red 71, Buddha reclined on a cot, an IV running into his arm. He blinked his eyes rapidly a few times, finally recognizing Cross.

"Everybody come home?" the pudgy man asked.

"They weren't fighters," Cross said, "just punks with guns. You were the only one who took a hit."

"Muñoz?"

"Same place as Humberto. It's all done."

"You're a real man, Buddha!" Rhino squeaked. "I'm sorry for everything I ever said bad about you. That was so brave, the way you covered Princess. . . ."

"I still don't see why that crazy bastard should get a share," Buddha mumbled as he drifted back to sleep.

♣

BUDDHA DREAMED he was sitting at a blackjack table in a lush casino. So Long was standing behind him, her jewel-lacquered nails over his right shoulder. He looked down at his two cards. Both aces: hearts and spades.

"Double down," the pudgy man said, just before he left his dream-state and dropped down to recovery-depth.

TWO TRAINS RUNNING

It is 1959—a moment in history when the clandestine, powerful forces that will shape America to the present day are about to collide. Walker Dett is a hired gun, known for using the most extreme measures to accomplish his missions. Royal Beaumont is the "hillbilly boss" who turned Locke City from a dying town into a thriving vice capital. Add a rival Irish political machine, the nascent black power movement, turf-disputing juvenile gangs, a muckraking journalist who doubles as a blackmailer, the FBI—and Locke City is about as stable as a nitroglycerin truck stalled on the railroad tracks.

Crime Fiction

ALSO AVAILABLE

Another Life
Blossom
Blue Belle
Born Bad
Choice of Evil
Dead and Gone
Down Here
Down in the Zero
Everybody Pays
False Allegations
Flood
Footsteps of the Hawk
The Getaway Man
Hard Candy
Mask Market
Only Child
Pain Management
Sacrifice
Safe House
Shella
Strega
Terminal

VINTAGE CRIME / BLACK LIZARD
Available wherever books are sold.
www.weeklylizard.com
www.randomhouse.com